# A Second Springtime

BY GORDON COOPER

THOMAS NELSON INC., PUBLISHERS
NASHVILLE      NEW YORK

Copyright © 1973, 1975 by Gordon Cooper

All rights reserved under International and Pan-American Conventions. Published by Thomas Nelson Inc., Publishers, Nashville, Tennessee. Manufactured in the United States of America.

*First U.S. edition*

Library of Congress Cataloging in Publication Data

Cooper, Gordon, 1932–
  A second springtime.

  SUMMARY: In the 1870's eleven-year-old Hester, who has lived in an English orphanage all her life, is adopted by a settler family in Nova Scotia.
  [1. Orphans—Fiction. 2. Nova Scotia—Fiction] I. Title.
PZ7.C7853Se4      [Fic]      75–2144
ISBN 0–8407–6428–6

FOR MY GOD-DAUGHTER AND NIECE

SARAH ELISABETH HUNT

# A Second Springtime

# *Chapter 1*

---

*T*HE BELL JANGLED in the housekeeper's room in the girls' wing of the orphan asylum at Marcroft.

"Monthly inspection over and done with," said Miss Fitch briskly. "We mustn't keep the visitors waiting."

Hester Fielding glanced at Bethanne Macey and smiled. Not much longer now, she thought, and then this last afternoon will be over. The two girls wore the regulation gray dress and black apron that formed part of the orphanage uniform.

Hester had been found in a basket outside the gates of the institution early one morning in March in 1862, eleven years ago. In the folds of the shawl in which she was wrapped there had been a piece of paper with the name "Hester" written on it in black ink. The matron, who was experienced in such matters, thought that the blue-eyed baby was about a month old and gave her the surname of

Fielding because there was no one else with that name in the records. Hester had grown up in the orphanage and was not unhappy, though for as long as she could remember there had always been bells and gray dresses.

Bethanne was the same age. She had come to the asylum when she was eight years old, and could remember a time when she lived with her mother and father in a cottage with a garden and an apple tree. Her father worked on a farm. One day he was gored by a bull and some men brought him home in a farm cart. Her mother ran out from the house and lifted the sack that covered his face. Then she cried for a long time.

Mrs. Macey and Bethanne had to leave the cottage because the farmer needed it for someone else, and they went to live in one room in a tenement building near the river, where Mrs. Macey tried to earn a living by making lace. In the winter there was an outbreak of fever, and Bethanne had a vague memory of pain and darkness, and the sound of footsteps and voices. Later she was told that her mother had died.

Someone had come from the orphan home, bringing a gray dress and a black apron, and she was lifted up into a cart and driven to the tall building. When the cart stopped outside the gates of the orphanage, she followed a woman in a black dress through echoing passages. Then a door opened into a room that seemed to be crowded with girls, each dressed in a gray gown and a black apron identical to those which she was wearing. Their hair was cut very short and Bethanne had suddenly thought of the time when she and her mother had gone to watch the sheep shearing in one of the barns at the farm where her father worked.

It was suppertime at the orphanage, and the girls stood

in two long lines down the length of a narrow table. The woman in black still went on walking, and Bethanne followed with her head bent, aware that the girls were looking at her. If she had looked up, she would have seen no enmity or spitefulness in their glances, but only a mild curiosity.

A place had been set for her at the far end of the table and she heard a woman's voice saying prayers. There was a clatter as the girls pulled back the benches and sat down to eat their supper of bread and cheese. A woman poured milk from a pitcher into the white mug that stood at each girl's place. Bethanne saw the bread and cheese, but she felt unable to eat anything because she was too tired and frightened. Then she became aware that the woman who had said the prayers was standing by her side.

"Eat your supper," the matron said, not unkindly, "and be thankful," and with hands that trembled, Bethanne took the food from the plate. When all the mugs and plates were empty, a bell rang and everyone stood up.

A fair-haired girl reached out for Bethanne's hand and they went up a flight of stone steps that led to the dormitory. "Your bed's next to mine," the fair-haired girl said. One of the bigger girls gave Bethanne a nightgown and she undressed. Then, as she lay in bed, she cried in loneliness and fear.

"You'll be all right, you'll see," the fair-haired girl said, although she knew that when a girl came to live in the asylum she cried for many weeks, especially at bedtime. In the morning she said, "My name's Hester," and she and Bethanne became friends.

Miss Fitch went to a cupboard and took out two white caps and gave them to the girls, who, under her watchful eye, had prepared the afternoon tea. When they had put them on, she stood looking at them for a moment and then nodded. "Right," she said. "Lead on, Hester."

"Yes, Miss Fitch," said Hester. She took a tray from the table, and, followed in single file by Bethanne and the housekeeper, she went out into the flagstoned passage that led to the matron's sitting room. She had often thought that the hardest part of serving tea to the wives of the orphanage guardians was the long walk to where the ladies were assembled. Once safely in the sitting room it was a comparatively simple matter to offer the dishes of muffins, plates of cake, and cups of tea to the guests. She looked down at the pink-and-white china on her tray, thinking how small the cups were, and so very different from the thick white mugs that were used by the forty-seven girls in the asylum. This is the last time that we shall serve the tea, she thought. A wave of excitement ran through her, and the cups rattled in the saucers.

"Take care, Hester," said the housekeeper.

"Yes, Miss Fitch," said Hester, and she took a deep breath to steady herself. As she walked past the door of the schoolroom that was presided over by Miss Blake, she could hear a hymn being sung by the girls who had not yet reached their eighth birthday. When the girl was eight she was expected to take her full share of all the duties in the institution, and then lessons ended at midday. In the afternoons the older girls took turns scrubbing the floors and working in the kitchen, the sewing room, and the laundry. The first time Hester had scrubbed one of the passages her arms had ached and her knees had been stiff, and even then she had been helped by a good-natured twelve-year-old girl who had already finished her own task.

Next to the schoolroom was the sewing room, which was ruled by Miss Brown. All was quiet as Miss Fitch and the two girls went by. No talking was permitted, and Hester knew that the girls would be sitting in silence around the big worktables, patching, darning, turning collars and letting down hems, waiting for the moment when Miss Brown would call them to her table so that she could inspect their work. Hester thought of the first lessons she had been given in the sewing room, remembering the sharp tongue and steel thimble of the instructress. In the past year she had progressed sufficiently to be entrusted with hemming the sheets and pillowcases which were sold to a dry-goods merchant who had a shop in the market square. Hester felt a sense of thankfulness when she reached the door of the matron's sitting room. Miss Fitch placed her tray on the table in the passage and then knocked on the door.

"Come in," said the matron.

Miss Fitch opened the door and Hester and Bethanne walked slowly to the end of the room with their trays and waited for the housekeeper to come in and begin pouring the tea. Lady Talbot sat in the most comfortable chair, a stiff figure wearing a purple mantle and an elaborately trimmed bonnet. Next to her were Mrs. Reed and Mrs. Clifford. Mrs. Henrietta Norton and her daughter-in-law sat together on a sofa. A chair from the housekeeper's room had been brought for the matron.

Hester looked at Mrs. Ruth Norton, thinking that it was not only the plain brown bonnet that made her seem so different from the other ladies of the inspection party. There was also the kindness in her gray eyes. Hester thought of the afternoon when she had spoken to the matron about the laundry, where the orphan girls were taught how to wash and iron in preparation for the day when they would be found a situation as a maidservant.

In addition to washing their own clothes, they also washed shirts for the thirty-nine boy orphans who lived in the male wing of the asylum, which was separated from the female wing by a high brick wall. At the far end of this wall there was a green door, which an usher unlocked once a week in order that four boys could come staggering through into the yard with the two big baskets that contained the shirts. In the laundry there were huge wooden tubs and mangles, and four copper pots that were so large that thirty pails of water were needed to fill each one to the brim.

When the girls first started working in the laundry they had handled only the orphanage clothes, but as the weeks passed, Mrs. Dowding, the instructress, allowed them to help with the articles that were sent in by the citizens of Marcroft, and then they washed and ironed nightshirts, sheets, and tablecloths, taking especial care when ironing that nothing was scorched or marked in any way.

"Is it necessary to have such large flatirons in the laundry, Matron?" Mrs. Ruth Norton said. "They must be extremely heavy."

"Mrs. Dowding is an excellent instructress," replied the matron. "I am sure that she takes great care to see that no accidents occur."

"I think that you may be worrying unduly, my dear," Lady Talbot said. "The girls here are being prepared for the time when they will go into service and will no longer be a burden on the taxpayers. We should be failing in our duty if we did not ensure that each girl was fully trained in all household tasks."

"But the girls are in our care," Mrs. Ruth Norton said earnestly.

"Exactly," Lady Talbot replied, "and so far the arrangements that have been made for their welfare have proved to be entirely satisfactory."

Mrs. Reed and Mrs. Clifford nodded in agreement, while Mrs. Henrietta Norton glanced anxiously at her daughter-in-law. Hester never forgot the look of sadness on the younger Mrs. Norton's face. I'm going to miss you, she thought, as she and Bethanne moved forward to serve the guests.

"Is everything ready for the girls who are going to Nova Scotia tomorrow, Matron?" said Lady Talbot, after she had accepted a cup of tea and a muffin.

"Yes, your ladyship," said the matron. "All the arrangements have been made in accordance with the instructions of the board of guardians. Miss Hayward, who will accompany the girls, will arrive late this evening. They will all leave on the eight-o'clock train to Liverpool in the morning."

Yes, thought Hester, everything's ready. Again the strange, excited feeling rose up in her, and she gripped the handles of her tray more tightly. She and Bethanne were two of the six girls who were leaving the orphanage the next day for a new life. Earlier in the year Mrs. Stewart, who was employed by a welfare agency in London, had appeared before a special meeting of the board of guardians and their wives and told them of how the agency had been able to arrange for orphan girls to be adopted by families who had settled in Canada.

"We have found," she said, "that first- and second-generation settlers are ready to offer a new opportunity to those less fortunate than themselves. The girls would have a full and happy life in new surroundings."

"The children in our care are very young to travel so far," Mrs. Ruth Norton had said doubtfully.

"They would be accompanied by an employee of the agency," said Mrs. Stewart, "who would ensure that each girl arrived safely at the home of the people who had agreed to adopt her."

"I am sure that it sounds most satisfactory," Lady Talbot had said. "We must always consider anything that would lighten the burden which our charitable institutions impose upon our citizens."

Her husband, Sir Henry, and the board of guardians thought so too, and the matron was instructed to prepare a list of the names of the girls who she thought might be suitable for adoption.

"The girls must have a genuine wish to go to Canada," said Mrs. Stewart. She sat in the center of the room facing the guardians and their wives and had not been in the least intimidated by the plumes on Lady Talbot's French bonnet. "Every girl would have to appear before the magistrates and state that she was willing to go. There must be no overpersuasion by those in authority." She looked at Mrs. Ruth Norton as she spoke, as if trying to reassure her. "In the past the agency has been able to place a number of girls in various parts of Canada. The reports we have received from time to time indicate that efforts to secure a new start in life for our orphans have met with considerable success."

"Thank you," Mrs. Ruth Norton had said, and her husband reached out for her hand.

The matron produced a list of six names, and Hester, Bethanne, Kitty Andrews, Ellen Holt, Mary Lewis, and Mercy Skinner were summoned to her room and listened as Mrs. Stewart and Miss Hayward from the welfare agency told them of the possibility that if they wished they could be adopted by families living in Nova Scotia.

"How could we get there, ma'am?" Mercy Skinner said.

"You would travel by train to Liverpool and then go by ship across the sea to Halifax. That would take about ten days," Mrs. Stewart said.

The girls glanced at each other. They had never made a journey by train. To travel by ship was something of which they had never even dreamed.

"Would it be like living here?" Mary Lewis asked.

"No," said Miss Hayward. "In Nova Scotia you would live in a house with a family."

"Would it be like it used to be, ma'am?" Bethanne said, and even Hester was surprised that she had asked a question. Bethanne was a quiet girl.

"Yes, my dear," Mrs. Stewart said gently. "It could be just like it used to be."

Bethanne had looked at Hester, and Hester knew that she was thinking of her father and mother, and of the time before she came to live in the orphanage. The other girls asked Mrs. Stewart and Miss Hayward some more questions, but Hester said nothing because she had no recollection of a life outside the walls of the asylum. She knew what the pattern of her life would be if she stayed in England.

When a girl was thirteen she was considered ready to leave the shelter of the institution. Efforts would be made to place her in a situation as a servant where she would receive board, laundry, and lodging, and a wage of one shilling each week, together with a promise from the employer that good conduct and service would entitle her to receive a small increase in wages at the end of the year.

It was not always possible to obtain posts for the girls in Marcroft in spite of the fact that it was well known in local circles that the training they received at the asylum turned them into excellent servants, and so sometimes they went to work in large houses as far away as London, where the wages were a little higher than they were in country districts.

The matron allowed the six girls two days in which to decide, and during the dinner hour they stood in a corner of the play yard and discussed the prospect of adoption.

"Imagine going in a ship," said Kitty Andrews.

"And not having to be in the sewing room with Miss Brown anymore," said Mercy Skinner, who had good reason to be afraid of the thimble finger of the sewing instructress.

Hester wondered what it would be like to live as a member of a family in a small house with perhaps a garden and an apple tree, as there had once been for Bethanne.

At the end of the two days all the girls told the matron that they would like to be adopted and go to live in Nova Scotia.

"You are all quite sure?" the matron asked.

"Yes, Matron," the girls said, and the matron informed the board of guardians and the clerk wrote to Mrs. Stewart.

A few days later the six girls walked to the town hall in the marketplace and stood in a line facing the three magistrates of Marcroft while the clerk to the board of guardians told the gentlemen that it would be of benefit to the taxpayers and to the girls themselves if they went to live in Nova Scotia. The magistrates nodded and stared at the six girls wearing black bonnets and cloaks who stood before them, and then asked each girl in turn if she really wished to emigrate. The girls were rather awed by the three gentlemen sitting on the high platform and they answered so quietly that Mrs. Ruth Norton, who was in the public gallery, leaned forward to hear what they said.

Finally the magistrates were satisfied and signed the certificates which authorized the girls' departure. The six orphans curtsied to the magistrates and walked out of the courtroom in single file. On the way Hester glanced up at the gallery and was surprised to see Mrs. Ruth Norton sitting there. Other people stared down at the six girls, and Hester thought that they must be some of the taxpayers who, she had been told so many times, supplied the food and clothing for the orphans in the asylum.

The arrangements for the adoption of the girls by families living in Nova Scotia were made by the welfare agency in London, and Mrs. Stewart wrote to the matron telling her of the plans that had been made. Hester was to live in a place called Silver Falls with a Mr. and Mrs. Clarke, and Bethanne would go to live with Mr. and Mrs. Gifford at Mapletown. Kitty Andrews would live in Halifax, and Ellen Holt, Mary Lewis, and Mercy Skinner were to travel farther inland.

The board of guardians sanctioned the making of a new dress for each of the six girls, and Miss Brown unrolled a bolt of gray material on her big worktable with a flush of excitement coloring her sallow complexion. She was not often asked to use her skill in cutting out new garments. The dresses were loose-waisted and were to be made with deep hems in the skirts, wide darts in the bodices, and broad tucks in the sleeves because it was a well-known fact that orphan children grew at an alarming rate.

Under Miss Brown's guidance the girls sewed quickly and carefully. She warned them of the dreadful consequences if the dresses were not ready by a certain date, and even Mercy Skinner, urged on by the threat of being left behind, stitched the long seams neatly enough to escape the flashing thimble of the sewing instructress.

There was a feeling of great relief in the sewing room when the six girls stood wearing the dresses for the very first time and were praised by the matron. Bonnets and cloaks were inspected and shoes repaired. Each girl would take with her a change of underclothes, a nightgown, and a comb wrapped in a black shawl.

When Mrs. Ruth Norton proposed that another dress and a second pair of shoes should be provided, Lady Talbot had considered this to be an unwarranted expenditure of taxpayers' money, but she agreed with the timid suggestion from Mrs. Clifford that each girl should be given a Bible, and the matron was instructed to purchase six from the bookshop in Church Lane.

Only Mrs. Ruth Norton glanced sympathetically at Hester and Bethanne as they moved among the guests with the muffins and slices of plum cake. Lady Talbot was in an affable mood and told the other ladies of how busy her daughter Miss Victoria was, preparing for her wedding. "So many fittings at the dressmaker's and visits to London, but then, it is essential that a young lady on the threshold of a new life should possess an extensive wardrobe," she said.

"Yes, indeed," said Mrs. Clifford.

"Dear Miss Victoria," said Mrs. Reed.

The tea party came to an end when Lady Talbot rose from her chair. Mrs. Ruth Norton smiled her thanks as Hester and Bethanne curtsied. "Good-bye, ma'am," Hester said to herself. The matron escorted the visitors to the front door of the home, and the two girls and Miss Fitch carried the heavy trays back to the housekeeper's room. Miss Fitch filled a kettle with water from a pitcher and placed it on the open fire to boil. As a small reward for the afternoon's work she always allowed her helpers to eat any food which was brought out from the matron's sitting room, and Bethanne and Hester shared one muffin and two slices of plum cake. Hester often wondered if Nan the cook thought it strange that nothing was ever taken back downstairs. The kitchen was considered by all the girls to be the best place in which to work, because it was the only room that was warm in the winter. Nan had grown up in the home but since she walked with a limp the guardians were unable to obtain employment for her, and so she had remained in the institution as a kitchen maid until she was appointed to the position of cook.

Miss Fitch poured herself a cup of tea from the visitors' teapot. Although it was no longer fresh, the quality of the tea served to the wives of the board of guardians was very different from that in general use at the asylum, and was kept in a special tea caddy in the matron's room. When the kettle boiled, Hester and Bethanne washed up the tea-things and put all the china away. Hester glanced at her friend as she closed the door of the cupboard and Bethanne's eyes flickered.

"Well," said Miss Fitch when the two girls had taken off their caps and stood waiting to be dismissed, "I hope that you find good places in Canada. You've been the best girls I've ever had to help me to wait on the visitors."

Hester and Bethanne smiled. Praise was rarely given in the orphanage.

"Off you go, then," said the housekeeper. "Miss Brown will be expecting you."

"Thank you, Miss Fitch," replied Hester and Bethanne.

"Come in," said Miss Brown, after Bethanne had knocked on the door of the sewing room. "Right," said the instructress when the girls went inside. "Get a needle threaded and make a start on that basket of stockings. I want them all neatly mended by suppertime. And I shan't tell you again, Mercy Skinner," she said angrily, as Mercy looked up from her work. "That seam has to be finished before you go off tomorrow, even if it means that you sit here until midnight."

"Yes, Miss Brown," said Mercy, wishing that her hands were cool and steady, but because it was the girls' last evening in England, not even the sharp words of the instructress could dim the feeling of excitement and anticipation that seemed to be everywhere in the high-ceilinged room. Hester went on darning stockings, but she was thinking all the time of Silver Falls and of Mr. and Mrs. Clarke.

# Chapter 2

*H*ESTER WAS AWAKE early the next morning. She lay in bed and watched the day brighten through the small panes of the uncurtained windows of the dormitory, thinking of the journey in the train and the voyage from Liverpool to Halifax in Nova Scotia. She thought again of Mr. and Mrs. Clarke, with whom she was going to live. Although they had never seen her, they were willing to take her into their home in Silver Falls, and she hoped that she would soon learn their ways and be able to please them.

She looked around the long dormitory at the white-washed walls and the small windows and at the figures of the girls who were still asleep beneath the gray blankets. Perhaps in Silver Falls she would have a room of her own. She glanced at Bethanne, who slept in the bed next to hers in the corner. She was awake, too, and Hester realized that she had also awoken early on this very special morning.

When Miss Fitch came into the dormitory and rang the

bell, Hester and Bethanne were the first two girls to run to the basins and the pitchers of cold water at the far end of the room.

Kitty Andrews was still asleep and Miss Fitch came to the side of the bed and shook her, saying, "You can't be late on this day of all days, Kitty Andrews. Now look sharp."

Kitty moved protestingly in the bed, but Miss Fitch whisked the blankets from her. "Be quick," she said.

After they had washed, Hester and Bethanne folded their blankets and placed them in the center of their mattresses and then began to dress. The gray material of the new dresses seemed rather stiff and prickly, but for the first time since coming to the home, they were wearing something that had never been worn by anyone else. As Hester laced up the newly repaired shoes she felt that already she was a different person.

When everyone in the dormitory had washed and dressed, they marched to the dining hall. Before they sat down to breakfast, the matron read a chapter from the Bible and said a prayer, just as she did every morning. This time she said an additional prayer for the six girls who were leaving the orphanage forever, and although Hester stood with her hands clasped and her eyes tightly shut, she felt the color rise in her face as if she knew that all the younger girls were staring at her.

There was porridge and bread and butter for breakfast, and she tried to be as calm as everyone else appeared to be. Old Nan had sent up freshly baked bread from the kitchen as a special farewell treat, not caring whether Miss Fitch would ask her what had happened to the two loaves that had been in the bread crock the night before.

After the meal the six girls went back upstairs to the

dormitory and wrapped their possessions in the black shawls that were part of the asylum uniform.

"I wonder who'll sleep in our places?" Hester said to Bethanne as they put on their cloaks and bonnets. For a moment they looked at the two beds and then followed the other girls down the stairs and along the passage to the matron's room, where Miss Hayward was waiting for them.

"Come in," said the matron after Ellen Holt had knocked on the door, and the six girls went into the room and stood in a line before her table.

"You have everything?" said the matron.

"Yes, thank you, Matron," said Ellen Holt.

"How smart you all look," said Miss Hayward, looking at the new gray dresses, which showed beneath the black cloaks. She glanced at the pale faces set in the black bonnets, and her kindness was rewarded by six shy smiles.

"Well, girls," said the matron, "the guardians have instructed me to tell you that they hope that you will be happy with the families who are prepared to offer you a place in their homes in a new country. Remember everything that has been done for you here in the asylum and be grateful for all that you have been given. In your new situation always be obedient and deserving, and be careful never to give your benefactors any cause to regret their charity."

"Yes, Matron," the girls murmured.

The matron looked down for a moment at the papers on her table. "It is also my wish—and the hope of everyone here in the home—that you will do well in Nova Scotia," she said.

"Thank you, Matron," said the girls.

"I think that's all," said the matron. "The carter will be waiting."

She and Miss Hayward stood up and Mary Lewis opened the door of the sitting room. The matron and Miss Hayward went out into the passage and the girls followed them to the front door of the asylum. Hester nudged Bethanne. Not only was the matron allowing them to leave by the front door, but she was actually escorting them, as if they were the wives of the guardians.

A cart from the workhouse farm was waiting by the front steps to take them to the railway station, and the girls climbed up into the back while Miss Hayward stood talking quietly with the matron. As Hester looked down from the cart she thought with some surprise that for all her authority, the matron was quite a small woman. It was her high cap and the chatelaine around her waist with its many keys that made her seem such a frightening figure.

Miss Hayward sat in the seat next to the driver.

"Good-bye, girls," said the matron, and her voice was rather indistinct, as if she had a cold.

"Good-bye, Matron," replied the girls dutifully, and they waved to her until the cart had passed the tall iron gates of the orphanage. They had never before seen the town of Marcroft at half past seven on a morning in May. The street sweepers were busy with their brooms, and housemaids wearing white caps and aprons and print dresses were polishing brass door knockers. A chimney sweep and his apprentice were just coming from the garden door in the wall surrounding Mrs. Henrietta Norton's house. The curtains in her bedroom were still drawn. She had not yet pulled the bell rope, indicating to the maid in the kitchen that she was now ready for her early-morning cup of tea. In the tenement buildings down by the river, the men had set out for their work at half past five and a lacemaker had already been working for three hours in order to finish some lace edgings that had to be at Miss Ward's shop in Lavender Road by nine o'clock. In the largest house in Marcroft, Lady Talbot slept in her four-poster bed, dreaming of mantles and gowns for her daughter Victoria.

Although the railway station had been built four years ago, it was the first time that any of the girls from the asylum had seen it. As she looked at the high red brick arches and dormer windows, Hester thought that it was not unlike a church. The orphans stepped down from the cart and followed Miss Hayward to the booking office, where she purchased seven tickets to Liverpool, and then they all went up a flight of broad stone steps to the platform to await the arrival of the train. Not many people intended to travel so early in the morning, and Miss Hayward and the six girls were able to sit together on a hard wooden bench. Hester glanced across to the other platform, where there was a large clock. It was five minutes to eight.

"There's Mrs. Ruth Norton," said Mercy Skinner suddenly. "I wonder where she's going."

But Mrs. Norton was not going anywhere by train. She had come to say good-bye. The girls stood up and curtsied.

"Good morning," said Mrs. Norton, smiling.

Miss Hayward looked at the figure in the plain bonnet and mantle. Mrs. Stewart had told Miss Hayward about young Mrs. Norton and her real concern for the orphan girls. "If only there were more people like her," she had said, thinking of some of the asylums and workhouses that she had visited.

"It's a lovely day for a journey," said Mrs. Norton. "Did you all have a good breakfast?"

"Yes, thank you, ma'am," said Ellen Holt, and the other

girls nodded and smiled in agreement. Mrs. Ruth Norton was so different from Lady Talbot and the wives of the guardians. She was someone with whom it was always possible to feel at ease.

"Well, just in case you were too excited to eat," said Mrs. Norton, "I've brought this." From beneath her mantle she took out a wicker basket in which there were some buns and seven oranges. The girls looked first at the basket and then at Mrs. Norton. The last time that they had seen oranges was on Christmas Day.

"Thank you, ma'am," said Ellen Holt.

When the train came into the station, the girls stared at the comfortably upholstered seats in the first- and second-class carriages. A woman in a large green bonnet glanced from the window of a first-class carriage at the row of six girls standing on the platform and idly wondered who they were and where they might be going.

"Marcroft station!" shouted a man, and then the doors of the railway carriages opened and porters hurried about with luggage. One climbed up a ladder on the side of one of the carriages and began to secure wicker baskets, traveling bags, and trunks to the luggage rack on the roof. Miss Hayward had bought third-class tickets and she and the six girls would travel to Liverpool sitting on wooden seats in a carriage in which there was no upholstery. She opened the door of the last carriage and the girls went inside and sat close together with their bundles on their laps. Mrs. Norton looked at the excited faces and then handed the buns and the oranges to Miss Hayward.

"God bless you," she said when the train began to move. She stood on the platform and waved until she could no longer see the train and then she walked slowly back to her house in King Street.

In their third-class carriage Miss Hayward and the six girls sat looking out of the window. Through her work for the welfare agency in London Miss Hayward had traveled to many parts of England, but to the girls, everything they saw was new and exciting.

As the train passed through the countryside, Hester looked at the green fields and at the hedgerows where the white hawthorn blossom was beginning to gleam, and for the first time in her life she was suddenly aware of the colors of spring. In the asylum there had been no garden in which the orphans could play, only the yard, and it was overshadowed by the tall, somber buildings. Hester wondered if there would be flowers in Silver Falls. As they passed farmhouses, they could see sheep and lambs, and Bethanne thought again of the cottage in which she had once lived with her father and mother.

At half past ten Miss Hayward gave everyone a bun and half an orange. "We'll have the rest later on," she said.

Hester thought how strange it seemed—to be looking out of the window of a railway carriage and to be eating a bun and half an orange. When the train stopped at railway stations along the route, other travelers entering the compartment glanced at the six girls in black bonnets and cloaks sitting with the plainly dressed middle-aged woman, and they were aware of a feeling of suppressed excitement that showed itself in the ready smiles of the girls and the flushed cheeks beneath the broad-brimmed bonnets.

It was just twelve o'clock when the train reached Liverpool. The railway lines had not always passed through green fields and the outskirts of market towns. Sometimes as the girls had looked out of the window, they had seen the tall chimneys of factories where men, women and children worked long hours for very low wages. The train had passed tenement buildings not unlike those by the river at Marcroft, where families lived in one room and rats ran among the litter in the streets. At Liverpool the railway station was considerably larger than that of Marcroft, and the girls followed closely behind Miss Hayward, who seemed quite untroubled by the noise of the engines and the large number of people on the platform.

"There's something to be said for traveling with only a modest amount of luggage," said Miss Hayward, looking at her small bag and the bundles which the girls carried. Hester glanced at the train where the porters were busily removing the luggage from the roof racks.

"I think we'll have lunch first," said Miss Hayward as they came out from the railway station, and she led the way into a small eating house where she chose a table in the corner and calmly ordered lunch for seven.

"Very good, madam," said the proprietress.

The girls were glad that their table was in the corner. Hester, Bethanne, and Kitty Andrews sat together on a high-backed settle and were hidden from the view of the occupants of the other tables. Hester thought how marvelous it would be to be as calm and assured as Miss Hayward. Everyone was hungry after the journey and they were quite ready for the boiled potatoes and meat pies that were brought to their table by a young Irishwoman.

"Will you be traveling far, ma'am?" she asked Miss Hayward.

"We're going to Nova Scotia," said Miss Hayward.

"Are you now?" said the waitress, looking around at the six girls. "Well, here's wishing you a safe and pleasant journey."

"Thank you," said Miss Hayward, and the girls smiled at the young woman who would have liked to have stayed talking for a little while longer, but she knew that the proprietress of the eating house was watching her. After the meal the waitress brought seven cups of tea, which was very hot and strong, and so very different from the tea at the orphan asylum. When Miss Hayward paid the bill, Hester wondered who had provided all the money for the train journey, the meal, and the sea voyage.

"Always remember that you are beholden to the taxpayers for the clothes you wear, the food you eat, and for the roof over your head," she had often been told, and she thought that it must have been the generosity of the taxpayers that had made the journey to Nova Scotia possible. As she went out from the eating house, she looked at the waitress who was carrying a tray of crockery back to the kitchen, and then she glanced at Bethanne and thought of the afternoons when they had served muffins and plum cake to the wives of the board of guardians in the matron's sitting room.

"We'll go to the dock now," said Miss Hayward, and the girls followed her along several streets until they came to the water's edge, where men were busy loading cargo onto a vessel.

"That's our ship," said Miss Hayward. "The *Annapolis Valley*."

It was a full-powered steamship with three masts and a single funnel, which had made its first voyage in September of the previous year, sailing from Liverpool to Halifax, and then to Boston and back again to Liverpool. The wife of the chairman of the shipping line was interested in the work of the welfare agency, and it was through her influence that Mrs. Stewart had been able to obtain cabin passages at very reduced rates for the six orphan girls and Miss Hayward.

"Well," said Miss Hayward, taking some papers from her bag, "this will be our home for the next few days."

The girls stared at the ship, and then they went up the gangway. Hester was again aware of Miss Hayward's calm manner as she spoke to the sailor who stood on the deck.

"Good afternoon, ma'am," said the sailor. "Show these young ladies to their cabin, Will," he said to a boy, "and be sharp about it."

"Yes, Mr. Bell, sir," said the boy.

"Thank you," said Miss Hayward, and they all went with the boy down several flights of stairs until he stopped outside a door.

"The six young ladies are in here together, ma'am," the boy said, "and you're on your own next door."

"Thank you, Will," said Miss Hayward, smiling. She opened the cabin door and looked inside. It was not very large. There was only a small standing space because most of the room was occupied by six berths, which were arranged in two tiers. A lamp was screwed to one of the ceiling beams, and there was a low shelf on which stood a metal jug and basin.

"Well, as you can see," said Miss Hayward, "there will not be a great deal of room for everyone, so I shall want you all to be as tidy as you can. Unpack now, and then we'll go up on deck. Kitty, Hester, and Bethanne can take the top berths."

When Miss Hayward opened the door of her own cabin, Hester thought that it was smaller than the cupboard in the housekeeper's room at the orphan asylum, but Miss Hayward seemed quite pleased.

The six girls soon unpacked. Nightgowns were placed

beneath the brown blankets on the berths, and everything else was tied back up in the black woolen shawls, which were then hung on the row of pegs on the back of the cabin door. Because there was nowhere to sit, Kitty, Hester, and Bethanne climbed up on to the top berths.

"We can touch the ceiling up here," said Kitty in surprise, and everyone laughed, thinking of the high-ceilinged dormitory at the orphanage.

"Well done," said Miss Hayward, when she came into the cabin and saw them sitting quietly. "The time is going on," she said. "We shall be sailing soon."

The six girls followed her up on deck and found an empty space at the ship's rail. All the cargo had been loaded and everything was in readiness for the time of departure. Hester did not know how many passengers were traveling on the *Annapolis Valley*, but a small group of well-wishers had gathered at the dock side to wave good-bye, and as she looked down at them, she thought of Mrs. Ruth Norton, who had brought fruit and cake for the train journey.

Orders were shouted and sailors hurried about on deck, and then slowly the vessel began to move. It was only when the expanse of water between the ship and the quay began to widen, that Hester really knew what her decision to go to Nova Scotia would mean. She was leaving everything that she had ever known in order to begin a new life in another country with people whom she had never seen. There had been the conversations with Mrs. Stewart and Miss Hayward in the matron's sitting room, the visit to the magistrates' court, and the excitement of making the new dress, but even then she had not fully understood what would happen.

Now, as she looked at the swirling gray water and the

receding huddle of the dock buildings, she knew that she was leaving England and the security of the orphan asylum forever. There could be no going back. She must accept whatever awaited her at Silver Falls. She glanced at Bethanne, who was standing by her side, and from the thoughtful expression on her friend's face it seemed that Bethanne, too, was thinking of the orphanage. She was also remembering her father and mother.

"We'll go below now," said Miss Hayward gently. As Hester turned to follow Bethanne, she looked at the upper deck, where other passengers had gathered. A clergyman and his wife and daughter were traveling to Boston. The cloak of the clergyman's daughter was deep blue, and beneath a matching bonnet her hair fell in long auburn tresses. Hester went down to the cabin thinking of her own hair, which was cropped short in accordance with the regulations of the asylum, and she wondered if there would ever come a time when it would be as long as that of the girl in the blue cloak and bonnet.

In the cabin the girls sat on their berths and Miss Hayward took out a storybook from her bag and read to them and in some way her calm, steady voice lessened the uneasiness that Hester had felt when she had stood at the rail of the ship looking down at the increasing expanse of water.

They had a meal of bread and cheese, which was brought from the galley at five o'clock, and they finished the last of Mrs. Norton's oranges and buns. Afterward the girls went up on deck and stared down at the sea as the ship moved farther away from England.

They went to bed early that evening, because Miss Hayward said that it had been a long, tiring day for everyone. In the upper berths Kitty Andrews was soon asleep, but Hester and Bethanne lay awake, not saying anything, but conscious of the roll and the throb of the ship as it steamed on through the night.

In the morning Miss Hayward came in to wake them.

"Hurry up, girls," she said. "Breakfast will soon be here."

"Oh, Miss Hayward," said Kitty Andrews. "I feel so bad. I think I must be dying."

"Nonsense," said Miss Hayward, but although she spoke briskly, her face was rather pale. "It's only the motion of the ship. What you need is plenty of fresh air. Get dressed as quickly as you can, and go up on deck."

All the girls were seasick. They felt so weak that they could hardly stand up, but slowly they dressed, helping each other with buttons and laces. When they went up on deck, as they took deep breaths of the bracing air, Kitty Andrews suddenly hurried to the rail of the ship. She was followed by Ellen Holt, and then by Bethanne.

"Are you feeling better now?" said Miss Hayward, and the girls smiled rather wanly.

"Does anyone want anything to eat?" asked Miss Hayward.

"Oh, Miss Hayward," gasped Kitty Andrews. "I never want to see another scrap of food for as long as I live."

"Well, I hope that you'll be able to change your mind soon," said Miss Hayward. She spoke cheerfully, although she knew that the seasickness could last for several days.

When it was time for lunch, none of the girls could eat anything, and they just lay in their berths, feeling weak and ill. No one spoke, but they were all thinking of the orphanage at Marcroft. There it would have been an unheard-of thing for any of the orphans to be lying on their beds in the dormitory at midday, but the gray walls they had known for so long seemed warm and comforting and so very far away. Hester thought again of Mrs. Ruth Norton, remembering how she had come to the railway station to say good-bye, and she also thought of the Sunday afternoons when the doctor's wife had sat in the dining hall and listened to the girls as they read from the Bible.

She felt so ill and faint as she moved restlessly in her berth, hearing the groans and whimpering of the other girls. A cold compress was placed on her forehead by Miss Hayward. Everything in the cabin seemed to dip and spin, until she fell asleep.

For three days the girls lay in their berths, unaware of the passing of the time. Then on the fourth morning, when Hester awoke and stared up at the ceiling planks of the cabin, although there was the same movement of the ship, she no longer had the dreadful feeling of sickness, and she realized with some surprise that she was quite hungry. She glanced at Bethanne, who was also awake.

"Do you feel any better?" Hester asked.

"Yes," said Bethanne thankfully. "I could eat a big breakfast."

"So could I, Bethanne," said Mercy Skinner from the berth directly below Hester.

Soon afterward Miss Hayward came into the cabin carrying a pitcher of water and two towels.

"Good morning, girls," she said, hoping that the seasickness had passed.

Everyone in the cabin was now awake, even Kitty Andrews, and they all greeted Miss Hayward cheerfully. Miss Hayward looked pleased. "I hope that everyone is feeling better," she said, looking at each of the girls in turn and seeing the color in their cheeks.

"Yes, thank you," the girls said, and the chorus of voices reassured Miss Hayward.

"That's good," she said. "Now, if everyone will wash and dress, I'll see about breakfast."

When Hester climbed down from her berth, she still felt weak, but when the breakfast came, she enjoyed the thinly-buttered toast and the cup of tea.

"Well, now," said Miss Hayward when the meal was over. "Go up on deck and get as much fresh air as you can."

The girls put on their bonnets and cloaks and went up on deck, where they were able to find a space well out of the way of the sailors. As she and Bethanne leaned against the rail of the ship, Hester was aware of the immensity of the sea and the sky. There was no land at all to be seen. Wherever she looked, there was only the cloudy sky and the gray-green water. She heard the sound of someone whistling and she turned and saw a sailor hurrying up a flight of steps to the upper deck. She wondered what it would be like to spend so much time at sea in the small, cramped quarters of a ship.

On Sunday morning a service was conducted by the clergyman who was traveling to Boston. It was held on the lower deck and was attended by all the passengers and most of the crew. It was the first time that any of the girls had seen the captain of the ship and they thought how splendid he looked in his dark-blue uniform. When the congregation sang the hymn, the captain's deep voice could be heard by everyone. The *Annapolis Valley* was really a cargo ship and it never at any time carried more than twenty passengers. Miss Hayward and the six girls stood in the back row of the congregation and Hester was able to see again the long auburn tresses of the girl in the blue cloak and bonnet. She wondered if Mrs. Clarke in Silver Falls would allow her to let her hair grow. Miss Hayward had said that the ship would reach Halifax on Thursday, and every evening Hester lay awake thinking of Mr. and Mrs. Clarke, knowing that every minute of every day was bringing the meeting nearer.

"I hope that you've enjoyed the voyage," said Miss Hayward after supper on Wednesday.

"Yes, thank you," said the girls.

"Now that the seasickness has gone," said Kitty Andrews, and the girls laughed and looked at each other. A day on board the *Annapolis Valley* had been so different from the days they had known at Marcroft. Bells still sounded at intervals, just as they had in the orphan asylum, but their message was only for the crew of the ship and not for its passengers. There were no instructresses to scold the girls for work which they considered had been badly done.

Every day on the ship had been like a holiday. They had their own special place on the lower deck where they read to Miss Hayward from their Bibles, and sometimes Miss Hayward told them stories. Hester thought how wonderful it must be to have read so many books, as Miss Hayward so obviously had. There had been very few books in the schoolroom at Marcroft. Talking had not been permitted in the dormitory at the orphanage, but during the voyage the girls had whispered in the darkness and Miss Hayward had never rapped on the wooden partition which divided her cabin from theirs, not even when Mercy Skinner laughed aloud at something Kitty Andrews had said.

On the last evening, as the girls undressed and climbed into their berths, there was very little conversation in the cabin. Now that the journey had nearly ended they would soon be meeting the people who were to be responsible for their future welfare and happiness.

"I hope they'll like us," said Bethanne suddenly, and although of all the girls she was the most gentle and shy, she was able to voice the thoughts of everyone.

# Chapter 3

THE NEXT MORNING the six girls went up on deck and stood at the ship's rail as the *Annapolis Valley* entered the port of Halifax. During the voyage they had seen only sea and sky, but now everything on the skyline was bright and colorful in the morning sunlight. Along the coast there were many sheltered bays with clusters of houses and small fishing boats, and on the horizon the girls could see the dark outlines of the forest. Gray and white sea gulls wheeled around the vessel or rode calmly on the water, quite unperturbed by the swell of the sea, and one stared up unwinkingly at the girls as they looked eagerly at everything. On the wharves of the port there were barrels of rum and molasses from the West Indies, and piles of timber from the lumberyards of Nova Scotia, which would be shipped to England. Beyond the docks the ground rose sharply to the town, and there were streets and squares and a church tower that gleamed in the sun.

Even the air is different, Hester thought. There was the sharp, sweet scent of timber mingling with the smell of tar and fish. Groups of men were waiting at the quayside. Most of them were wearing dark trousers and navy-blue shirts, but two wore plaid jackets and Hester remembered that Miss Hayward had said that Nova Scotia meant "New Scotland." She looked down at them, thinking that perhaps Mr. Clarke had come to meet her and was wondering at that moment which of the six girls was Hester Fielding.

"Well, here we are," said Miss Hayward, who had also come up on deck and was standing behind the girls. "It's time to go down to the cabin now. Pack up everything and make sure that it's left neat and tidy. We shall be able to leave the ship in about twenty minutes."

When the girls went below, they looked with affection at the six berths in the small cabin and wondered where they would be sleeping at the end of the day. When the last knots had been tied in the six black shawls, the girls waited until Miss Hayward was ready and then they all went up on deck. The holds of the ship were being opened, and as the men who had been waiting on the quayside came up the gangway to unload the cargo, the girls thought of what might be contained in the large bales and packages that were piled on the deck.

"Ready?" asked Miss Hayward, and two by two the six girls followed her down the gangway to the quay. From the upper deck the clergyman and his wife looked at the plainly dressed woman and at the black bonnets, cloaks, and shawled bundles of the girls, and then the clergyman's wife gently touched the long auburn tresses of her daughter, who was cradling a wax-faced doll in her arms.

Hester thought how strange it seemed to be walking on land, after having grown accustomed to the roll of the ship, and she was aware of the noise her newly repaired shoes made on the cobblestones. In the immigration shed Miss Hayward opened her bag and gave some documents to one of the officials. When all the formalities were over, the man looked at the six faces framed by the black bonnets.

"Welcome to Canada," he said.

"Thank you, sir," said Ellen Holt, and the other girls smiled. Then Miss Hayward led them through the port gates and out into the street. An elderly, red-faced man was standing by a horse and cart.

"Miss Hayward and the six young ladies from England, ma'am?" he asked.

"Yes," said Miss Hayward, smiling.

"I'm to take you to the Reverend Weston's house in Lockmore Street," said the man.

"Thank you," said Miss Hayward.

"Will there be any more luggage, ma'am?" said the man, glancing at Miss Hayward's bag and the six bundles.

"No," replied Miss Hayward. "We have everything with us."

The girls climbed into the back of the cart and Miss Hayward sat with the driver in the front seat. The narrow street rose steeply away from the dock and as the cart moved slowly uphill, the girls looked at the buildings and the people. Men were pushing carts piled with goods toward the docks, and sometimes it was difficult to pass because of the narrowness of the street. Some of the houses

*43*

were small and built of wood, but others were made of stone, with broad-silled windows and wide front doors. A woman in a blue gown was cleaning the windows of her house and she raised her hand in greeting as the cart went by. When they came to the top of the hill, as the girls looked back they could see the masts of the ships in the harbor, and Hester wondered if any of the vessels might soon be returning to Liverpool. The man drove the cart to a quiet street and stopped outside a small, stone-built house, and before Miss Hayward stepped down from her seat, the front door opened and Mr. Weston and his wife came out.

"Good morning, Miss Hayward," said the minister. He helped her down from the cart, while his wife stood smiling at the girls.

"Good morning, sir," said Miss Hayward, curtsying.

"You had a good crossing, I hope?" said Mr. Weston.

"Once the seasickness passed," said Miss Hayward, thinking of the first few days of the voyage.

"And these are your charges," said Mr. Weston. "Welcome to Halifax."

The girls were still sitting in the back of the cart and so were unable to curtsy to the minister, as Miss Hayward had done. They smiled shyly, and Hester thought that Mr. Weston was very different from the vicar of Marcroft, whom she had only seen in church on Sunday mornings when he was wearing a cassock, a white surplice and a richly embroidered stole. Mr. Weston wore a dark coat and trousers and a fawn waistcoat. He held out his hand to Bethanne and helped her down from the cart, and then he did the same for Hester and the other girls.

"Thank you, Dan," he said to the driver.

"You're welcome, Reverend," said the man, and he

raised his whip in a kind of salute to everyone and then drove away.

"Now come along inside," said Mrs. Weston kindly. She was plainly dressed in a black gown and a white cap and apron, and Hester remembered the jet-trimmed mantle and the beribboned bonnet worn by the vicar's wife at Marcroft.

The girls placed their bundles on a table in the hall and then Mrs. Weston led them along a narrow passage to a low-ceilinged room at the back of the house. It was plainly furnished with a large dresser, two chairs, a bench, and a scrubbed table. Arranged on the shelves of the dresser there were pewter plates and some white cups and saucers. On the windowsill there was a fern in a brightly polished brass pot.

"I hope that you're all ready for a bowl of soup," said Mrs. Weston. She went to the fireplace, where there was an iron cooking pot suspended from a chain, and began to ladle soup into bowls for her guests. There were also thick slices of freshly baked bread, and when everything was ready, Mr. Weston said the grace and then Miss Hayward and the girls sat down at the table to the meal.

The minister and his wife spoke kindly to their visitors. They asked them about the voyage and were anxious to make everyone feel at ease, but in spite of their kindness there was an undercurrent of apprehension in the room as the girls sat thinking of the settlers who had offered them a home. When the meal was over, they went into the garden while Miss Hayward and Mr. Weston sat in the minister's parlor discussing the arrangements that had been made for the safe arrival of each girl.

Mr. Clarke would be in Halifax at half past twelve to take Hester to his home in Silver Falls. Bethanne would also go with them and Mr. Gifford would be waiting in Silver Falls to take her on to Mapletown. Mr. and Mrs. Clancy lived on the outskirts of Halifax and would call at the minister's house at two o'clock for Kitty Andrews. Ellen Holt, Mercy Skinner, and Mary Lewis were to travel to towns farther inland, and they and Miss Hayward would spend the night in the Westons' house and set out early the next morning.

Apple trees had been trained against the walls of red brick that enclosed the garden. Everything in it was neat and orderly. Mrs. Weston loved her garden, just as she did each room of the house in Lockmore Street. Close to the house there were rosemary bushes and a few early spring flowers, and then there was a bed of herbs separated from the vegetable garden by a low hedge of lavender. At the end of the garden there was a well and a long, low bench where Mrs. Weston often sat with her needlework in the summer. There was just room enough for the six girls to sit down, and they sat looking at the windows of the house, each thinking that merely to sit and wait was the hardest thing of all. Hester thought that her heart was beating very rapidly, and she wondered if Bethanne could hear it.

"What do you think they're doing back at Marcroft?" said Ellen Holt suddenly.

"Thinking about lunch, I expect," said Mary Lewis.

"I'd rather have Mrs. Weston's soup," said Kitty Andrews quickly, and they all laughed. For a few moments at least, the laughter helped to dispel the uneasiness of the girls. Mercy Skinner stopped biting her nails, and Bethanne was able to sit with her hands clasped less tightly in her lap. Then they saw Mrs. Weston coming along the path, and they glanced at each other and stood up respectfully.

"Let me show you my herb garden," Mrs. Weston said, and she began to tell the girls the names of each plant and the reason for its place in the garden. She spoke gently and calmly, and her kindness had the same effect as the laughter. Hester hoped that there would be a garden at the back of the Clarkes' house in Silver Falls. Then she realized that Miss Hayward was standing by the back door.

"Has someone arrived, Miss Hayward?" said Mrs. Weston.

"Yes," said Miss Hayward. "It's Mr. Clarke for Hester and Bethanne."

"Well, now," said Mrs. Weston, "which is Hester and which is Bethanne?" but she knew by the tremulous smiles on their faces who the girls were for whom Mr. Clarke was waiting.

"Good-bye, my dears," she said.

"Good-bye, ma'am, and thank you," Hester and Bethanne murmured. Mrs. Weston kissed them, and after they had said good-bye to the other girls, Hester and Bethanne followed Miss Hayward into the house, both wishing that they could stay forever in the garden with Mrs. Weston. Miss Hayward opened the door of the parlor and the two girls went inside. Hester felt herself trembling and she clenched her hands beneath the folds of her dress in an attempt to steady herself. Bethanne stood beside her, with her eyes downcast.

"This is Hester Fielding, Mr. Clarke," said Miss Hayward, touching Hester on her right shoulder.

"Pleased to meet you, Hester," said a man's deep voice.

Hester looked at the man who had risen from a straight-backed chair by the fireplace and now stood smiling down at her. He was heavily built and seemed very tall in the small room. He was wearing a thick, dark jacket and trousers, and in his hand he held a fur hat. His black beard was lightly touched with flecks of gold, and his eyes seemed very blue against his sun-tanned skin.

"Thank you, sir," said Hester, her voice trembling slightly.

"So you're going to be our girl," said Mr. Clarke.

"Yes, please, sir," said Hester humbly. She curtsied as gracefully as she could and then stood waiting for Mr. Clarke to speak.

"Mrs. Clarke and Ben have been looking forward to this day," said Mr. Clarke. He looked questioningly at Mr. Weston and then at Miss Hayward, who stood just inside the room, behind the two girls. As Hester curtsied, there was a sudden, sharp pricking in Miss Hayward's eyes.

"And this is Bethanne Macey," she said as briskly as she could, "who will be going to Mr. and Mrs. Gifford."

"Hello, Bethanne," said Mr. Clarke. "Mr. Gifford lives some distance from Silver Falls, so it's been arranged that you should come with us to my place, and he will be waiting there to take you on home."

"Thank you, sir," said Bethanne. She felt Miss Hayward's hand on her shoulder and took a step forward and curtsied, just as Hester had done.

"Well," said Mr. Clarke, "if the girls are ready, I'd like to be making a start back to Silver Falls."

"Yes, they're quite ready," said Miss Hayward. "Get your things," she said to Hester and Bethanne, and after the two girls had taken their shawled bundles from the table in the hall, everyone went out into the street, where a horse and buggy were waiting by the hitching rail. Mr. Clarke put the two bundles in the back of the buggy, next to a small barrel and a coil of rope.

"There's room for both of you up front," he said to

Hester and Bethanne. "Happen you'll be able to see more from there."

Miss Hayward went to the front of the buggy as the girls settled themselves in the front seat.

"You'll soon settle down," she said encouragingly. "Good luck."

"Thank you, ma'am," Hester and Bethanne said.

"God bless you," said Mr. Weston, and then Mr. Clarke climbed into the driving seat.

"Off we go, then," he said, and the buggy began to move. Hester and Bethanne looked back and waved to Miss Hayward and Mr. Weston until the buggy went around a corner and they could no longer see them. The two girls glanced at each other, both feeling a moment of fear as they realized that they were now alone in the buggy with Mr. Clarke, but he smiled reassuringly at them.

As they passed through the streets of Halifax, he pointed out places of interest to the girls. They liked especially the town clock, which had been installed in 1803 by the order of the Duke of Kent, and they thought how imposing Province House was. When Mr. Clarke told them that it was there that the laws of Nova Scotia were administered, Hester remembered the time when she and Bethanne and the other girls had stood before the magistrates in the town hall at Marcroft, and Mrs. Ruth Norton had been sitting in the public gallery.

After they had left the town of Halifax, they came into the open country, where on both sides of the road there were fir, hemlock, spruce, and maple trees. In some places the ground had been cleared of timber, and wooden farmhouses had been built. Beside them there were barns and outbuildings, and in the fields herds of brown-and-white cattle were grazing. Sometimes they passed through small villages that seemed to Hester to nestle on the very edge of the dark forest. They drove for a long time through thickly wooded countryside which was often scarred by deep ravines where the red earth was strewn with rocks and pebbles. Sometimes as the buggy jolted along the rough road Hester and Bethanne could see deserted log cabins standing on tracts of land that had once been cleared by the early settlers, but which had since been repossessed by the surging bracken and brambles. It was late in the afternoon when Mr. Clarke said "We're just coming into Millford now. Silver Falls is another eight miles from here."

Not much farther now, Hester thought, and then I shall see Mrs. Clarke and Ben. She wondered if Ben was Mr. and Mrs. Clarke's son. She glanced at Bethanne and she knew that she was thinking about Mr. Gifford, who would be waiting for her in Silver Falls.

At Millford there was a stone-built church and narrow streets of houses. As they drove through the main street, they passed a schoolhouse and an inn. On the bank of the river there was the mill that had given the town its name. The sun gleamed on the water and Hester thought of the pewter plates on the dresser in the kitchen of the minister's house. A dog lay in the sun by the blacksmith's forge, and he sprang up and barked as the buggy went by. Hester thought how big the dog was, and she felt glad that she was sitting next to Mr. Clarke. On the outskirts of Millford there were more isolated farmhouses, and she wondered if the people who lived in them were ever lonely. She looked again at the dark, silent forest, and in spite of the warmth of the spring afternoon and the sheltering folds of her rough cloak, she shivered.

"Cold, lass?" said Mr. Clarke.

"No, sir," Hester said quickly, but Bethanne had been looking at the wooded hills, which stretched as far as anyone could see, and she knew why her friend had shivered. It was as if the forest were waiting for someone. Mr. Clarke drove steadily on and Hester thought that the horse must be getting tired because they had traveled such a long way. Since leaving the town of Millford they had been able to see the river as it wound and twisted through the low-lying pastures, and suddenly Mr. Clarke pointed to a waterfall and said, "That's how the township of Silver Falls got its name. We'll soon be home now."

The girls had never before seen a waterfall and they sat smiling at its beauty. As the water poured down into the lower reaches of the river, it gleamed in the sunlight and Hester thought that the cascade seemed almost like a drift of snow. When they drove into Silver Falls, Mr. Clarke showed them the lumberyard where he worked, and Hester and Bethanne could see great tree trunks that had floated down the river from the logging camps up in the hills. Set some distance back from the road there was a church and a small graveyard enclosed by a picket fence. A few of the cottages were built of stone, but most of the small houses were made of wood. There was a general store and an inn called The Apple Tree. An old man was sitting on a bench on the sidewalk and he called out in greeting as the buggy went by.

"Afternoon, Eli," said Mr. Clarke, and Hester and Bethanne knew that the old man was staring curiously at them.

"The schoolhouse is down that way," said Mr. Clarke, pointing to a side road. "It's easy to find one's way in Silver Falls."

They drove past some more houses and then the sidewalks ended and they began to pass meadows that were bright with spring flowers. By the side of the road there was a board on which had been painted the words "Pollitt's Spread," and a cart track led to a farmhouse with outbuildings and an orchard of apple trees.

"The Pollitts are the nearest neighbors we have," said Mr. Clarke. "You'll be seeing Mrs. Pollitt before long, I expect." He looked down and smiled at Hester, and although everything was so different from what she had always known, because of his kindness Hester was able to smile back. She wondered if Mrs. Pollitt had seen the buggy pass by.

"And this is our place," said Mr. Clarke after a few minutes. He drove from the main road along a narrow cart track that led to a wooden house. A horse and buggy stood by the hitching rail. A boy was sitting on the front porch, and when he saw Mr. Clarke and the two girls, he jumped up from his chair and went to the front door. A woman in a faded blue dress came out, followed by a man wearing a dark-brown jacket and a fur hat.

"Here we are, then," said Mr. Clarke. "All safe and sound."

The woman came down the steps of the porch, smiling at the two girls in the front seat of the buggy.

"I'm Mrs. Clarke," she said. "Which of you is Hester?"

"I am, ma'am," Hester said.

"You're very welcome," said Mrs. Clarke. She gave her hand to Hester and helped her step down from the buggy.

"And you must be Bethanne Macey, then," Mrs. Clarke said to Bethanne. "Mr. Gifford's here waiting to take you on to his place." She helped Bethanne down from the buggy, and the two girls stood side by side. Then the man in the fur hat came down the steps.

"How do you do, young lady?" he said to Bethanne.

52

"Very well, thank you, sir," Bethanne said, her voice trembling slightly.

"Pleased to make your acquaintance, Mr. Gifford," said Mr. Clarke.

"Much obliged to you for all your trouble," said Mr. Gifford, and the two men shook hands.

"It was no trouble at all," said Mr. Clarke. "There was no point in two of us driving all the way into Halifax, and the girls were company for each other."

"You and Mr. Gifford have quite some way to go," Mrs. Clarke said to Bethanne. "But you've time enough to step inside for a drink of milk."

"Thank you, ma'am," said Bethanne, and the two girls went with Mrs. Clarke into the house. In the corner of the room a baby was lying in a wicker cradle.

"His name's Davy," said Mrs. Clarke. "He's asleep now, but you can go across and look at him."

Hester and Bethanne went over to the cradle and looked down at the baby. In spite of the strangeness of everything, they smiled when they saw him because he looked so peaceful and defenseless.

"Now come and sit yourselves down," said Mrs. Clarke, "and have that milk."

When the two girls came to the table they saw that as well as two mugs of milk, there was a plate of bread and butter.

"Have something to keep you going until suppertime," Mrs. Clarke said kindly.

"Thank you, ma'am," said the girls. They were hungry after the long journey from Halifax. As she began to eat, Hester looked around the room. There was a stove on which stood two big black kettles and a large iron saucepan. The stove chimney was black and shiny and through it the smoke from the wood fire was drawn outside. On the shelves of a dresser there were tin plates, a clock, china dishes, and thick mugs hanging from hooks. An oil lamp stood next to a box of cutlery, and a second lamp was suspended from one of the ceiling beams. The floor was of scrubbed boards, and bleached sacks served as rugs. By the stove there was a rocking chair with a brown cushion on it. In one corner of the room there was a ladder that led up to a loft. Hester suddenly felt that someone was looking at her, and when she turned, the boy was standing on the threshold with the two shawled bundles.

"This is my son Ben," said Mrs. Clarke.

"Hello," said Ben quietly, putting the two bundles in the rocking chair.

"Hello," said Bethanne and Hester. They had never before spoken to a boy.

Mr. Gifford was standing by the door. "We'll be setting off as soon as you're ready," he said to Bethanne.

"Yes, sir," Bethanne said. She took another sip of the milk and wondered if there would be time enough for another piece of bread and butter.

"Have some more to eat, Bethanne," said Mrs. Clarke, smiling at the two girls.

"Thank you, ma'am," said Bethanne.

Mrs. Clarke waited until the mugs and the plate were empty. Then she said, "Well, now, say your good-byes in here and then come out when you're ready." She looked at Ben, who followed her out onto the porch, and then Mrs. Clarke closed the door quietly behind her.

"They'll not be a minute," she said to Mr. Gifford.

Inside the house, Hester and Bethanne still sat at the table.

"I wish that we could stay together," Bethanne said softly.

"You'll be all right," Hester said, just as she had on Bethanne's first evening at the orphan asylum.

They both tried to smile.

"Perhaps we might be able to come visiting one day," said Hester.

"Yes," said Bethanne. Tears were in their eyes, and they held hands for a moment, trying to comfort each other, and then Bethanne went over to the rocking chair and picked up her bundle.

"Good-bye," she said.

"Good-bye, Bethanne," said Hester.

"All right, young lady?" asked Mr. Gifford, when the two girls went out to the front porch.

"Yes, sir," said Bethanne. "Thank you, ma'am, for your kindness," she said to Mrs. Clarke.

"You're very welcome," replied Mrs. Clarke.

"I'm obliged to you both," said Mr. Gifford.

"Glad to have been of help," said Mr. Clarke. He held Bethanne's bundle while she stepped up into the front seat of the buggy. Hester stood on the porch, thinking how forlorn Bethanne seemed as she sat next to Mr. Gifford with the bundle on her lap. She bit her lip as the buggy began to move.

"Safe journey," said Mr. Clarke.

"Good-bye, Bethanne," Hester called out.

"Good-bye, Hester," said Bethanne.

As her friend drove away with Mr. Gifford, Hester waved until the buggy had gone down the cart track and passed out of sight. Then, as she looked at the garden and the apple trees, she knew that she was now completely alone, a stranger in someone else's house, a stranger in a new country.

"Come on inside, Hester," said Mrs. Clarke, "and I'll show you the rest of the house."

"Yes, ma'am," Hester said obediently, but her voice trembled.

"You can hang your bonnet and cloak on one of the pegs by the window," said Mrs. Clarke.

Hester found that her hands were shaking as she untied the strings of her black bonnet, but when she took it off there was a sudden spurt of laughter from Ben.

"Ben," said Mrs. Clarke sternly.

"Sorry, Ma," he said.

"You'd better go and see if you can help your father," said Mrs. Clarke, and Ben, his face very red, hurried out through the back door. Hester knew that Ben had laughed because her hair was cut even shorter than his. She looked at Mrs. Clarke. Her auburn hair was almost the same shade as that of the clergyman's daughter on the *Annapolis Valley*. It was gathered into a knot, and Hester thought that when it was combed it would probably reach to her waist. Mrs. Clarke came over and helped her to take off her cloak, and Hester stood in the gray dress that was really too big for her, with its deep hem and the tucks in the sleeves. Mrs. Clarke looked down at her, thinking of the time when the fair hair would be long enough to be tied with a ribbon.

"You mustn't pay any attention to Ben," she said. "I expect that we'll all be a bit shy of each other until we've settled down."

She placed the bonnet and cloak on one of the wooden pegs and then she showed Hester the rest of the house. In addition to the living room there was a small pantry where her provisions were arranged neatly on the shelves. On the floor there was a bread crock made of brown earthenware, and two large pitchers of water, each with a muslin cover. The other two rooms were the bedrooms of Ben and his parents. In Ben's room there was a chest of drawers and a bed with a dark-brown counterpane on it. A fishing rod was hanging on the wall, next to a picture of a tree.

"Ben did the drawing," said Mrs. Clarke, looking at Hester and smiling reassuringly.

On the bed in the other room there was a patchwork quilt which Hester thought was the most beautiful thing that she had ever seen. It was made from so many colors, and because of their glory the room seemed warm and cheerful.

"That was a long time in the making," said Mrs. Clarke, pleased at the admiring expression on Hester's face. On the wall by the window, placed so high that only Mr. Clarke would be able to reach it, there was a gun. There was a chest of drawers, and a table on which stood a green-and-white jug and basin.

"Your room is up in the loft," said Mrs. Clarke when they went back into the living room. Hester took her bundle from the rocking chair and followed Mrs. Clarke up the ladder. In the loft there was a bed with a faded pink quilt spread on it, and a low chest where clothes could be kept. On a shelf there was a blue vase with a few yellow flowers in it. A sharp, sweet smell came from the rafters.

"You can keep your things in here," said Mrs. Clarke, opening the lid of the chest, so Hester placed the bundle on the bed and began to untie the knots in the shawl. Lady Talbot had considered that ample provision had been made for each girl, but when the underclothes, the night-gown, the comb, and the Bible were spread out on the pink quilt, Hester realized that the contents of the bundle were very few. She knew that because she had come to live in Silver Falls, she would no longer be dependent upon the taxpayers of Marcroft for her food and clothing. She would be a burden on Mr. and Mrs. Clarke instead. There was a strange expression on Mrs. Clarke's face as she looked at Hester's belongings.

"This dress is new, and I had my shoes mended before I came, ma'am," Hester said. Her face reddened and she looked at the floor, afraid that Mrs. Clarke might be angry because there had been so little in the bundle.

"You look very smart," said Mrs. Clarke gently. She put the underclothes into the chest and the nightgown under the pillow, and Hester placed the comb and the Bible on the shelf next to the yellow flowers.

"Do you like the color gray?" asked Mrs. Clarke.

"Yes, thank you, ma'am," said Hester.

"If you'd like a change, I've some brown dye out in the barn," said Mrs. Clarke, "and I think you can find something in the ragbag, and then we can put a colored braid on the skirt. Would you like that, Hester?"

"Yes, please, ma'am," said Hester. She wondered if Mrs. Clarke knew that she had never worn anything other than the gray uniform of the orphanage.

"You can keep your shawl in the living room," Mrs. Clarke said, so Hester took the black shawl from the bed and then they went down the ladder.

"I hope that you're going to be happy here with us, Hester," Mrs. Clarke said. "We've all been looking forward to your coming."

"Thank you for taking me in, ma'am," said Hester. There was an aching feeling in her throat and she was afraid that she was going to cry.

"We want you to think of this as your home," said Mrs. Clarke. "And I'd like you to call me Ma, and you must call my husband Pa."

"Thank you," Hester said.

Mrs. Clarke looked in the cradle and smiled when she saw that Davy was still asleep.

"Do you know very much about babies, Hester?" she asked.

"No, ma'am," said Hester.

"You'll be able to help me look after Davy," Mrs. Clarke said. "You'll soon learn. Well, now that you've seen everything inside the house, we'll go and see what there is out the back."

On the back porch two pitchers of milk had been set to cool in a tub of water. A short distance from the house there was a barn, a cow shed, and a stable. They were all separate buildings, set apart from each other in order to lessen the risk of an outbreak of fire. In the stable was the horse who had drawn the buggy all the way from Halifax. She whinnied in greeting when Mrs. Clarke and Hester went up to the stall.

"Her name's Blackie," said Mrs. Clarke. "Because of her coat."

In the barn Mr. Clarke and Ben were chopping wood. When Mrs. Clarke and Hester went inside, Ben looked up and then went on with his work. Seeing him there, Hester was again aware of her cropped hair, but Mr. Clarke looked kindly at her and then glanced at his wife.

"I'm just showing Hester everything that there is to see," said Mrs. Clarke.

"That's right," said her husband. "Get acquainted with everything and everybody."

Hester and Mrs. Clarke stayed in the barn for a little

while and then they went outside into the yard. A cow was grazing in a small field, and Mrs. Clarke told Hester that her name was Maggie.

"Ben always does the afternoon milking," she said, "but now that you're here, you'll be able to learn. Would you like that, Hester?"

"Yes, Ma," said Hester, although she thought that the cow seemed very big and she wondered if Maggie would like being milked by her after being accustomed to Ben. When they went back into the living room, Davy was awake and as Hester stood by the cradle, he looked back up at her with eyes that were blue like Mr. Clarke's. Mrs. Clarke brought a saucepan of potatoes from the pantry and put it on the stove. When she lifted the lip of the other saucepan, there was an appetizing smell of stew.

"Sit in the rocking chair, Hester," said Mrs. Clarke.

"Thank you, Ma," said Hester. She sat rocking gently as Mrs. Clarke set the table for supper. Everything was ready when Mr. Clarke and Ben came in from the barn. After Mr. Clarke had said grace, Mrs. Clarke and Ben murmured, "Amen," but Hester spoke up as clearly as if she had been at the home, and she thought how loud her voice sounded in the room, which was so much smaller than the dining hall at Marcroft. Although she was nervous and sat with her eyes downcast, she was hungry and she enjoyed the stew and the boiled potatoes. Afterward Mrs. Clarke poured tea from a brown teapot into thick white mugs.

"Do you like your tea sweetened, Hester?" she said.

"No, thank you, Ma," Hester said, because there had never been any sugar in the tea at the orphanage.

"Ben's a sweet tooth," Mrs. Clarke said, and she put a spoonful of molasses into his mug. After supper Mr.

Clarke and Ben went out to work in the barn, and Mrs. Clarke said that she would get Davy ready for bed.

"Shall I wash the dishes, Ma?" Hester said. She wanted to do something to show Mrs. Clarke that she was grateful to her for her kindness.

"Thank you, Hester," Mrs. Clarke said. She brought an earthenware basin and a dishcloth from the pantry.

"You'll find a tea towel in the top drawer of the dresser," she said, and then she took Davy into her bedroom. Hester filled the basin with water from the kettle and then began to wash the supper things. She had dried everything and was putting the tin plates back on the dresser when Mrs. Clarke said, "Is everything all right, Hester?"

"Yes, Ma," Hester said.

"Well done," said Mrs. Clarke. "You can come into the bedroom while I sing Davy to sleep."

Hester sat on the floor while Mrs. Clarke sang to Davy. Sometimes she looked at the cradle where Davy lay, but she also glanced at Mrs. Clarke as she sat on a stool in her faded blue dress, singing the words of an old lullaby.

When Davy was asleep, Mrs. Clarke and Hester went back into the living room. Mrs. Clarke showed Hester where the teapot and the basin of dishwater could be emptied on the garden by the front porch, and then she sat down at the table with her workbasket. On the top there was some gray flannel which she said was to be made into a shirt for her husband. She gave Hester a needle and thread and asked her to sew a button on a shirt belonging to Ben. Hester hoped that she would be able to thread the needle at the first attempt so that Mrs. Clarke would not be impatient, as Miss Brown so often was.

In the sewing room at the asylum, anyone who took too

long to thread a needle was rapped on the head with a thimble and scolded for wasting time. Although her hand trembled slightly when she took the needle and thread from Mrs. Clarke, Hester was able to thread the needle quite easily, and when she looked up again she realized that Mrs. Clarke was not wearing a thimble. After the button had been sewn on the shirt, Hester sat hemming a tea towel while Mrs. Clarke went on sewing the gray flannel. As they worked, Mrs. Clarke told Hester that she and her husband had been living in Silver Falls for fourteen years.

"We sailed from Liverpool and landed at Halifax, just as you did," she said, thinking of the early days in Nova Scotia. The price of the land was higher than she and her husband had thought it would be, and they realized that the little money they had saved would not go very far. In order to acquire the sum needed for the first payment on a holding of land, Mr. Clarke had gone to work in one of the logging camps farther inland, and Mrs. Clarke had found work in a lodging house in Halifax. The work at the lodging house was hard, but the owner and his wife liked and trusted her. As the weeks passed, she carefully saved her small wages, and although she was often lonely and homesick, she consoled herself by thinking of the time when she and her husband could be together. They had been married two weeks when they sailed from Liverpool, and she remembered her feelings of homesickness and fear when her husband had set out for the logging camp, knowing that it would be at least six months before they were able to see each other again.

A year later the land at Silver Falls had been chosen and Mr. Clarke began clearing the ground so that a one-roomed house could be built and crops sown. The wife of the owner of the lodging house gave Mrs. Clarke a mattress, two blankets, a saucepan, some cutlery, and an oil lamp, and when Mr. Clarke came for her, she drove off in a hired buggy with him, feeling as rich as Queen Victoria in England.

They worked hard, and after more land had been cleared of trees, stones, and undergrowth, a barn and cow shed were built and another room was added to the wooden house. Mr. Clarke obtained work at the newly established lumberyard in Silver Falls. He was away all day and did not come home until suppertime, and often Mrs. Clarke was lonely, but then Ben was born and she knew that she would never be lonely again.

Through the years the Clarkes prospered. More land was cleared, a stable was built, and then the house was enlarged. At last the day came when they had finally paid for the land, and they stood on the back porch looking at the outbuildings and the three fields, feeling a great sense of thanksgiving for their good fortune and not remembering the hardship and privation that they had known.

At eight o'clock Mrs. Clarke said, "Bedtime for you now, Hester."

"Yes, Ma," Hester said. She immediately stood up and folded her work neatly, just as if she had been in the sewing room at the orphanage.

"I'll come up in a few minutes," said Mrs. Clarke, as Hester went up the ladder to the loft. Hester undressed and put on her nightgown and then knelt down and said her prayers. As she lay in bed waiting for Mrs. Clarke, she remembered the long dormitory at Marcroft and the small cabin on the *Annapolis Valley,* and she thought how strange it seemed to be in a bedroom by herself. When Mrs. Clarke came into the loft, she tucked the bedclothes around Hester and kissed her.

"Good night, Hester," she said.

"Good night, Ma," Hester said softly.

After Mrs. Clarke had gone down into the living room, Hester lay thinking about Mr. Clarke and Ben. Then she thought of Bethanne, and she wondered if the Giffords had a baby like Davy, and if Mrs. Gifford was as kind and welcoming as Mrs. Clarke.

"Good night, Bethanne," she said, and tears came into her eyes.

# Chapter 4

*F*OR A MOMENT, when she awoke the next morning, Hester was not quite sure where she was. Then, as she lay in bed looking up at the rafters of the loft, she realized that she was here in Silver Falls and that the Clarkes would be downstairs in the living room. She pushed back the bedclothes and went to the window and looked out at the barn, the stable, and the cow shed. Maggie was in the small field and beyond that there was another meadow and a field of green corn. On the far side of the river the forest stretched away into the distance, silent and mysterious. Because she did not know what time it was, Hester went back to her bed and pulled the sheets and blankets around her, and soon afterward Mrs. Clarke came up into the loft. "Good morning, Hester," she said.

"Good morning, Ma," said Hester.

"Did you sleep all right?" asked Mrs. Clarke.

"Yes, thank you, ma'am," said Hester.

"Pa is at work," said Mrs. Clarke, "and Ben's gone off to school. You've slept on this morning. It's nearly nine o'clock."

Hester felt guilty at having overslept. She moved uncomfortably in the bed and hoped that Mrs. Clarke would not think that she was a lazy and an idle girl.

"It's a fine, blowy day," said Mrs. Clarke. "It will be a good chance for me to see about your dress. You can wear a shirt and a pair of Ben's trousers while it's being dyed." She put the shirt and trousers on the bed and looked down at Hester.

"Ben's clothes?" said Hester wonderingly.

Mrs. Clarke laughed at the expression on her face. "Well, the trousers are too small for him, and I had put them away for Davy," she said, "but it'll be quite a few years yet before he's ready for them. Get dressed and then you can come down and wash in my room, and then we can see about some breakfast."

Hester put on the shirt and trousers, and although the shirt was too big, the trousers seemed to fit quite well. She was glad that Ben and Mr. Clarke would not see her until later in the day, when the strangeness of wearing a boy's clothes had lessened. She took the gray dress from the top of the chest and went down the ladder into the living room and stood rather uncertainly by the table.

"You look quite smart, Hester," said Mrs. Clarke.

"Thank you, Ma," Hester said. She laid the dress over the back of the rocking chair and went into Mrs. Clarke's bedroom, where she washed her face and hands in cold water from the green-and-white jug on the table. The bed had already been made, and she glanced again at the bright colors of the patchwork quilt before she went back into the living room. For breakfast there was a bowl of porridge, bread and molasses, and a mug of milk. At the orphanage there had sometimes been bread and treacle, and Hester thought that the taste of the molasses was very similar.

After breakfast, while Hester washed the dishes, Mrs. Clarke brought the green-and-white basin into the living room and began to bath Davy, and when the dishes were done, Hester stood by her chair, ready to hand the towel and then the baby's clothes to Mrs. Clarke.

"Would you like to hold him for a minute or two?" said Mrs. Clarke, and Hester sat in the rocking chair nursing Davy while his mother carried the basin of water outside and hung the towel on the clothesline. Hester felt rather nervous holding Davy, but he looked up and once she thought he smiled at her, and then Mrs. Clarke brought the wicker cradle into the living room and placed Davy in it.

"Well, now," she said, "I'll see about your dress, Hester. While I'm doing that, will you make your bed and tidy your room? You'll find a broom out on the back porch."

"Yes, Ma," Hester said. After she had made her bed and swept the floor of the loft, she looked out of the window. Mrs. Clarke was walking toward the barn carrying one of the kettles. The orphanage uniform was over her arm and with the last sight of the gray dress, Hester thought that her new life had really begun.

She took the broom out to the back porch and then came into the living room and sat in the rocking chair, but it seemed wrong to be doing nothing. She wondered if Ben's bed had been made, and she opened the door of his room and looked inside. Everything was neat and tidy. She looked again at the picture of the tree on the wall, and she thought how lifelike it seemed. Then from the window she saw Mrs. Clarke coming from the barn, so she quickly went back and sat in the rocking chair again, not wanting Mrs. Clarke to think that she had been prying.

"I've put the dress in the dye tub," said Mrs. Clarke. "I always think that brown is a warm-looking color." She took a ragbag from one of the row of pegs by the window and put it on the table. "Perhaps you'll be able to find something in here that we can use for the braid on the skirt, Hester."

"Yes, Ma," said Hester. She sat at the table and untied the drawstrings of the black ragbag and began to take out the pieces of material that were inside. There was some gray flannel very similar to that which Mrs. Clarke was using for her husband's shirt, and pieces of old blankets, toweling, and remnants of cotton print. Although some of the pieces were quite large, others were very small and could be used only for patchwork. As Hester was looking at the material, there was a knock on the front door. When Mrs. Clarke opened it, a tall, thin woman dressed in black was standing there.

"Good morning, Mrs. Pollitt," Mrs. Clarke said. "Come on inside."

"Thank you kindly," said Mrs. Pollitt. "I've just come over to see if that girl of yours has got here safely. I must have been over at the Robbs' place when Mr. Clarke drove by yesterday afternoon." She came into the room and stared at Hester, who looked shyly at her, holding a piece of gray flannel in her hand.

"Well, I never," said Mrs. Pollitt. "Did they send a boy instead?"

Hester felt her cheeks redden as she stood up, conscious of her short hair and the shirt and trousers.

"No," said Mrs. Clarke. "This is Hester. I'm just freshening up a dress for her, that's all."

There was a slight reproof in her voice, and Mrs. Pollitt pursed her lips.

"Well, anybody could make a mistake," she said. "Dressed up in a boy's clothes and all." But Hester knew that it was not only the shirt and trousers that had made Mrs. Pollitt think that she was a boy. It was also her cropped hair. Mrs. Pollitt stared at her, as she stood looking down at the piece of gray flannel in her hands.

"Come over here and let me look at you, then, girl," she said gruffly, and Hester left the flannel on the table and stood in front of her with her hands behind her back. Mrs. Pollitt tilted Hester's chin upward and looked down into her face.

"Put your tongue out," she said, and Hester did as she was told.

"I expect that you feel better after that," said Mrs. Pollitt. "All right, you can put it back again. You'll do. Get plenty of Mrs. Clarke's good victuals down inside you, and after a month or two you'll be nicely filled out."

"Yes, ma'am," Hester said, and she went thankfully back to the table.

"How's the Robb baby?" asked Mrs. Clarke.

"I reckon he'll be all right," said Mrs. Pollitt. "The better weather's coming on now. I always say that the best time of the year for a baby to be born is in the spring, then he's got the summer and fall before him." She went across to the cradle and looked at Davy, and Hester thought that he might be frightened by her big black bonnet, but there was a surprisingly gentle expression on Mrs. Pollitt's lined red face.

"If they were all like you, Davy," she said, "folk wouldn't be sending for me very often. Still, I always did say that this side of Silver Falls was the healthiest spot there is. I raised my own two sons here, anyway." She turned back again to Hester. "Mind that you keep well, young woman," she said.

"Yes, ma'am," said Hester.

"Well," said Mrs. Pollitt. "I'm pleased to have made your acquaintance. Once you've settled yourself in here with Mrs. Clarke, you must come over and visit me at Pollitt's Spread."

"Thank you, ma'am," said Hester, although she was not sure that she would enjoy calling on Mrs. Pollitt.

"See that you do," said Mrs. Pollitt, as if she knew what Hester was thinking. "That's what neighbors are for."

She and Mrs. Clarke went outside and stood talking on the front porch, while Hester continued to search through the contents of the ragbag. It was a new experience for her to be able to choose something for herself, and there were several pieces of material that she liked.

"Well, now you've met Mrs. Pollitt," Mrs. Clarke said when she came back into the living room. "Here in Silver Falls a great many folk have cause to be thankful to her. People always send to Pollitt's Spread when there's illness at home."

"Is there no doctor in Silver Falls, Ma?" asked Hester, thinking of Dr. Norton at Marcroft.

"No," said Mrs. Clarke. "But Mrs. Pollitt can always ask Dr. Hall to come out from Millford. Perhaps one day, when times get better, we'll have our own doctor right here in Silver Falls." She looked at the pieces of material that were spread out on the table. "Have you found anything that you like?" she asked.

"Could I have this, Ma, please?" Hester said. She held up a yellow remnant.

"You've made a good choice," said Mrs. Clarke. "Yellow and brown go well together—just like the leaves in the fall."

At twelve o'clock they had bread and cheese, and Hester had a mug of milk. Mrs. Clarke explained that the main meal of the day was supper, when everyone was at home. "When you go to school on Monday with Ben," she said, "you'll take your lunch with you, because it's too far to come home at midday."

In the afternoon she cut the yellow material into narrow strips and Hester sat hemming each piece while Mrs. Clarke went on with her shirt making. Once she looked at Hester's sewing and praised her small, neat stitches, and Hester thought of Miss Brown and her thimble in the sewing room of the asylum.

Ben came home from school at half past three.

"Did school go all right?" asked Mrs. Clarke.

"Yes," said Ben. "I'll be glad when I can leave, though."

"Now, Ben," Mrs. Clarke said. "You know that Pa wants you to have as much schooling as you can get. We're lucky to have a teacher like Miss Foster down at the schoolhouse."

Ben said nothing, but looked at Hester. She felt uncomfortable as he stared at the shirt and trousers.

"Even though Hester hasn't been to school today, she's been working for most of the time," said Mrs. Clarke. "Would you like to show her the river and the forest, Ben?"

"There's the milking to do," said Ben.

"That can wait for a little while," said Mrs. Clarke. "It's surprising what you can see in a few minutes."

Hester had finished hemming both sides of the narrow yellow strips. "You've done well," said Mrs. Clarke. "You can join them all together to make one long trimming later. Now, off you go with Ben."

Hester put her needle and thread into Mrs. Clarke's pincushion. She knew from the way that Ben was looking at her that he did not really want to take her with him.

"Come on, then," he said, and they went through the yard to the small field where Maggie was standing by the gate.

"She knows that it's near milking time," Ben said, and Hester thought that the cow looked reproachfully at her when, instead of opening the gate, Ben climbed up over the fence and began to walk to the other end of the field. Hester scrambled up over the fence, too, thinking with some surprise that she was glad that she was not hampered by a long-skirted dress, even if Mrs. Pollitt had thought that she was a boy. She had to run in order to keep up with Ben, but even then he walked a little way in front of her, not saying anything.

At the end of the field there was a gate into the big meadow and Hester hoped that Ben would open it, but instead he climbed over the fence and she knew that he would expect her to do the same. This time he looked back as she balanced precariously on the top of the fence, and she was glad when she jumped safely down onto the grass. The river ran at the end of the meadow, and when Hester and Ben reached the bank, Ben picked up a thin, smooth pebble and sent it skimming across the water.

"Ever been fishing?" Ben asked.

"No, Ben," Hester said.

"It's a good place for trout," said Ben. Six large, flat stones had been set to form a path right down to the water's edge.

"Pa put those there for when we go swimming," Ben said. "Can you swim?"

"No," said Hester. She realized that Ben would think that she knew very little. She wanted to tell him that she could sew and knew how to wash and iron clothes, but she thought that he would not be impressed by that. She wondered if it was Mr. Clarke who had taught Ben to swim and fish. Ben seemed to be so clever. He could do anything.

Across the river there was a bridge made of logs and she followed Ben across it to the edge of the forest. Spruce and balsam fir rose high into the sky, and there was the scent of pine. Fronds of bracken waved gently in the cool air beneath the interlacing branches of the trees, and Hester thought how mysterious everything seemed in the dim half-light.

"That's all there is to see," said Ben. "There's the milking to do." When they came back into the small field Maggie was still waiting by the gate and she turned her head as Hester and Ben came toward her.

"All right, Maggie," Ben said, as he opened the gate. Hester again thought how big Maggie was, and she stood back and waited for the cow to follow Ben into the cow shed. Hester's dress was hanging on the clothesline in the yard. It was no longer the uniform gray, but a deep shade of brown, just as Mrs. Clarke had promised. As Hester looked at the dress, Mrs. Clarke came out onto the back porch.

"Do you like the color, Hester?" she said.

"Yes, thank you, Ma," said Hester smilingly. "Shall I finish off the sewing?" Now that she had seen the new color of her dress, she wanted the trimming to be ready for Mrs. Clarke.

"Certainly," said Mrs. Clarke. "It's been a good drying

day and I'll be able to iron the dress after supper. I'll give it a good airing and then put the trimming on tomorrow, so that you can wear it for the first time on Sunday."

Hester went on with her sewing until there was a long yellow braid ready to be stitched onto the skirt of her dress. Ben came in for a kettle of hot water so that the milking pail could be scoured and then Mrs. Clarke began to make the supper. While she prepared a fish which Mr. Clarke had caught in the river, Hester peeled the potatoes and then set the table ready for the meal. When Mr. Clarke came home from work, he smiled when he saw that Hester was wearing a shirt and trousers, but Hester was able to smile back, not minding at all now about having to wear Ben's old clothes until her dress was ready.

After supper Mrs. Clarke put two flatirons on the stove and then took Davy into her bedroom, while Hester began to wash the dishes hoping that while Mr. Clarke and Ben were in the room she would not drop anything. She was glad when they went outside. When all the dishes were done and everything had been put away, Mrs. Clarke called her into the bedroom and Hester sat on the floor and listened as Mrs. Clarke sang to Davy.

When he was asleep, Mrs. Clarke went out into the yard and brought Hester's dress in from the clothesline. "Well, what do you think, Hester?" she said, smiling as she placed the yellow trimming about six inches above the hem of the skirt.

"It's lovely, Ma," Hester said, longing for the time to come when she could wear it.

She wore the dress for the first time on Sunday afternoon to church. When she came down the ladder from the loft into the living room, for a moment she felt as self-conscious as she had when she was wearing Ben's shirt and trousers.

"That's a fine-looking dress, and a fine-looking girl inside it," said Mr. Clarke.

"Thank you, sir," said Hester, and she went over to the row of pegs for her bonnet and cloak, glad that she would not disgrace the Clarkes in front of the people at church. Mrs. Clarke's Sunday dress was dark green. She had washed her hair on Saturday evening and it gleamed like burnished copper. Everyone went to the afternoon service. Ben sat with his father in the front seat of the buggy, and Hester sat with Mrs. Clarke and Davy in the back.

As they drove down to Silver Falls, Hester thought of churchgoing in Marcroft. On Sunday mornings the female orphans, led by the matron and surveyed by Miss Brown and Mrs. Dowding, walked to the parish church. Sometimes they saw the carriage in which Sir Henry and Lady Talbot rode on their way to the red-curtained pew that bore the Talbot coat-of-arms, and everyone, even the matron, curtsied respectfully. Lady Talbot would nod graciously and pass by on her way to church with an even greater sense of well-being. The orphans entered the church by a side door and sat in the north transept, from which they were unable to see either the altar or the pulpit. If any of the girls dared to look across the nave, they could see the boys from the male wing of the orphan asylum sitting in the south transept with the master and the ushers.

The fashionable congregation of the town sat in the front central pews, and sometimes Hester had glanced across at the bonnets and mantles of the Marcroft ladies and their daughters and wondered if, when she was grown up, she would ever have a bonnet with trimmings and bows of ribbon. Most of all she enjoyed listening to the organ. The music was everywhere, reaching even to the shadowed pews where the orphans sat, and it was able to cheer the hearts and minds of all who listened.

On Sunday afternoons the girls read from the Bible to Mrs. Ruth Norton, and she had never appeared to mind when they stumbled over a hard word, unlike Miss Blake, the week-day teacher, who never allowed a mistake to pass without making a caustic remark, or giving the offender a rap on the knuckles with a ruler.

It seemed strange to be able to ride to church in a buggy. Hester glanced at Davy. He was asleep, nestling against the folds of Mrs. Clarke's gray cloak. Mr. Clarke stopped outside the church for Mrs. Clarke and Hester to step down from the buggy and then he and Ben drove over to the hitching rails by the picket fence. When Hester followed Mrs. Clarke into the church, she thought how light and airy it seemed. There were no dark oil paintings or stained-glass windows. Light came in through the clear panes, and the spring sunshine was gleaming on the scrubbed wooden floor and the unvarnished pews and benches. A plain wooden cross stood in the center of the altar. A large black Bible rested on a wooden lectern, its scarlet bookmark the only touch of bright color in the entire building. A young woman was playing the organ.

Although there was no marble chancel floor, no shining brass, and no embroidered altar cloth, Hester felt that the simplicity of the whitewashed walls and the unvarnished wood was in itself a thing of beauty. She sat in a pew near the back of the church with Mrs. Clarke and Davy, listening to the organ as the people of Silver Falls began to assemble for the service. She recognized the old man who had been sitting on the sidewalk when she and Bethanne had driven through the main street with Mr. Clarke on Thursday afternoon. I wonder if Bethanne is sitting in a church somewhere, she thought, and Kitty and the other girls.

The bonnets and cloaks worn by the women and girls of the congregation were plain and made in dark, serviceable shades of brown, gray, and green. The men's jackets were made of thick cloth and their heavy shoes sounded noisily on the floorboards. Mr. Clarke and Ben came in and sat in the pew with Mrs. Clarke and Hester, and then Mrs. Pollitt walked up the aisle to one of the pews near the front of the church. She was followed by two young men, both of whom wore dark-gray jackets, and Hester thought that they were Mrs. Pollitt's two sons.

It seemed to her that no one stayed away from church. Small children, not yet old enough to go to school, held the hand of an elder sister, and babies, warmly wrapped in shawls, were carried by their mothers. Hester looked at the boys and girls, thinking that she would meet them at school the next day.

Mr. Anderson, the minister, stepped out from the front pew. He wore a frock coat, and Hester thought that he looked more like a magistrate than a clergyman. His hair was very white and his deep, resonant voice reached easily to the back of the small church. Hester enjoyed the service, feeling a sense of belonging as she joined in the singing of the hymns. Everyone was united in a simple faith. There was no pulpit, but Mr. Anderson stood in the aisle and spoke simply and directly to the congregation. During the singing of the last hymn a collection was taken and Mr. Clarke placed a coin on the wooden alms dish for the whole family. When the service was over, the minister walked to the church door and stood ready to shake hands with the people as they came out.

"And this is our new lassie, is it, Mrs. Clarke?" he said.

"Yes, Pastor," Mrs. Clarke said. "This is Hester," and Hester curtsied as deeply as she would have done if the vicar of Marcroft had ever spoken to her.

"There now," said Mr. Anderson kindly. "You've come to a grand place in a brave new country. I hope that you will be happy here."

"Thank you, sir," Hester said, remembering that at the parish church in Marcroft, when the morning service was over, the orphans from the home left the church by the same side door through which they had entered, and the vicar had never been waiting there to wish them good-bye.

No one stayed talking for very long outside the church in Silver Falls because there was the afternoon milking to be done, but the two Pollitt brothers spoke to Mr. Clarke and grinned at Hester and Ben. George and Luke Pollitt were not as tall as Mr. Clarke, but they were dark and broad-shouldered. Hester wondered what it would be like living at Pollitt's Spread with Mrs. Pollitt. When Mr. Clarke drove past the entrance to the church, Mrs. Pollitt was speaking to the minister's wife, who was wearing a bonnet and cloak of dark blue. Mrs. Pollitt raised her hand in greeting as Hester and the Clarkes went by in the buggy, and remembering the last time that they had met, Hester was sorry that Mrs. Pollitt could not see the glory of the brown dress with the yellow trimming.

That evening after supper, Mrs. Clarke asked Hester to sing Davy to sleep, and although Hester was pleased that Mrs. Clarke had asked her, she was afraid that the baby would begin to cry when he realized that it was not his mother sitting on the stool by his cradle, and she also knew that her voice would not be as true and sweet as Mrs. Clarke's. She began to sing softly, and then found that she could remember only the first three lines of the lullaby.

78

Davy did not seem at all tired. He lay watching her, his blue eyes wide open. Hester thought that Mrs. Clarke might come in and ask her why she had stopped singing, so she began to sing one of the hymns she had learned at the asylum. In the living room the Clarkes could hear her singing, and Mrs. Clarke glanced at her husband.

"What's she singing that for?" said Ben.

"A hymn is as good a song as any, Ben," said Mrs. Clarke. "Perhaps Hester doesn't know any others. You'll have to teach her some."

Hester sang three hymns before Davy went to sleep, then she tiptoed from the room and closed the door.

"Is Davy asleep, Hester?" asked Mrs. Clarke.

"Yes, Ma," Hester said thankfully.

"Come and sit by me, then," said Mrs. Clarke, "and I'll teach you the rest of the lullaby."

By the end of the evening Hester knew all three verses of the song. When she was in bed, Mrs. Clarke came up to the loft to tuck her in and wish her good night.

"School tomorrow," she said.

"Yes, Ma," said Hester. After Mrs. Clarke had gone back down the ladder into the living room, Hester lay thinking about the next day and the boys and girls she had seen in church and who would be at school tomorrow. She touched her hair. Remembering how Ben had laughed when she had taken off her bonnet, and that Mrs. Pollitt had thought that she was a boy, she wished that she could wait until her hair had grown.

# Chapter 5

*H*ESTER AWOKE EARLY the next morning and she lay in bed thinking about going to school. There was no clock in her room. Everything was very quiet and she wondered what time it was. Then in the living room downstairs she could hear Mrs. Clarke raking out the ashes from the stove, and then there was the sound of the back door opening and the noise of Mr. Clarke's footsteps as he went across the yard to the cow shed.

After the quiet Sunday a new working week had begun. Hester thought of the other children who would be at school and she wondered if they would know that she was a girl who had come to Silver Falls from an orphan asylum in England, or if they would think that perhaps she was a relative of the Clarkes who was now living with them. She remembered that Mrs. Pollitt and Mr. Anderson knew all about her, and when she thought of how small the village of Silver Falls was, she realized that everyone would know that she was not related to either Mr. or Mrs. Clarke. She thought again of her short hair, and of how Ben had laughed.

Since she had arrived at the Clarkes' house, she had spent most of the time with Mrs. Clarke, helping her in the house. Everyone in the household had specially allotted tasks. Before he went to work each morning, Mr. Clarke milked Maggie and after supper he worked in the garden or was busy in the barn. Ben did the milking in the afternoon and brought in a basket of wood for the stove. He also cared for Blackie, cleaned the stable, and attended to the harness.

Hester remembered the afternoon when Ben had shown her the fields and the river, and she knew that he had taken her with him only because Mrs. Clarke had asked him. Perhaps he was angry because I was wearing some of his clothes, she thought. When Mr. Clarke had finished milking Maggie, Hester heard him come back across the yard to the house for breakfast and later on there was the sound of the front door closing when he went off to his work at the lumberyard. Then she went to sleep again and did not wake until Mrs. Clarke called out to say that it was time to get up. Hester pushed back the bedclothes and dressed. When she went down the ladder into the living room, Mrs. Clarke was by the stove preparing the breakfast.

"Good morning, Hester," she said.

"Good morning, Ma," Hester replied.

"Would you like to wash before you have breakfast?" asked Mrs. Clarke. "Ben's not up yet."

"Yes, Ma," Hester said. She went into the big bedroom and poured some water from the green-and-white jug into the basin, hoping that the sound of the water would not awaken Davy, who was asleep in the cradle. The water was cool and refreshing against her skin. After she had re-buttoned her dress, she emptied the water from the basin into a pail and left everything ready on the small table for Ben.

When she went back into the living room, Mrs. Clarke placed a bowl of porridge before her and poured out a mug of milk. "I'm glad that there's one early riser in the house," she said.

"Thank you, Ma," Hester said and she began to eat her porridge. Everyone had been up early at the home, and she had found it no hardship to get up as soon as Mrs. Clarke called her. Ben was still not up, and Mrs. Clarke went to the door of his room and said quite sharply, "Now, I shan't tell you again, Ben. You'll be late, so come on."

"All right, Ma," said Ben sleepily. He came out from his bedroom and went into his parents' room to wash. Mrs. Clarke began to cut slices of bread from a round loaf. She made two piles, each of four slices, and then placed a piece of cheese on the top slice. From one of the drawers in the dresser she took out two pieces of blue-and-white-checked cloth and made two bundles of the bread and cheese.

"That's the lunch for you and Ben," Mrs. Clarke said, "and there'll be stew for supper tonight."

After Hester had finished breakfast, she went up to the loft and made her bed. As she combed her hair, she wondered if the children at school would laugh at her, just as Ben had. At the orphanage none of the girls had laughed at anyone else, because everyone had cropped hair and they all wore the same gray uniform. When she went down the ladder into the living room, Ben was eating his porridge.

"Good morning, Ben," she said softly.

"Morning," said Ben, and went on with his porridge. Hester glanced at the clock on the dresser, thinking that it would be terrible if they were late for school, especially on her very first day. After Ben had finished eating his porridge he had a slice of bread and butter before he pushed his chair back from the table.

"Ready?" he said.

"Yes, Ben," Hester replied.

Ben took his cap from the first peg and Hester put on her bonnet and cloak. Her fingers trembled as she tied her bonnet strings and the bow she made was slightly crooked. Mrs. Clarke went over and straightened the ends of the bow, and then gave Ben and Hester their lunch bundles.

"Off you go, then," she said.

"Good-bye, Ma," said Ben.

"Good-bye, Ben," said Mrs. Clarke. "Good-bye, Hester."

"Good-bye, Ma," said Hester.

Mrs. Clarke stood on the porch as they set off for school. Although they walked side by side, neither of them spoke. Hester hoped that Ben would say something, but he walked purposefully on with a grim expression on his face. When they reached the gate they both turned and waved to Mrs. Clarke before going out onto the road. When they could no longer be seen from the house, Ben began to walk much more quickly so that Hester had almost to run in order to keep up with him. Suddenly he stopped and said, "She's not your ma, and she never will be," and then he ran off down the road.

His angry words made the color rise in Hester's face. In the few days that she had been in Silver Falls, in spite of the kindness and sympathy of Mr. and Mrs. Clarke, she had been aware of the unfriendliness of Ben. It was not only because of the way in which he had behaved out in the fields by the river, but there had been his silence on the few occasions when the two of them had been alone in the living room. Often Hester had wanted to say something to break the sense of uneasiness that she felt, but she thought that any overture of friendship should be made by Ben. Although the Clarkes wished her to call them Ma and Pa, it seemed that Ben had no intention of thinking of her as a sister. When his parents had told him that they were thinking of giving a home to an orphan girl from England he had said, "Why can't it be a boy?"

"A girl would be company for me, Ben, when you and Pa are out on the land or in the forest," said Mrs. Clarke. "Besides, wouldn't you like to have a sister?" And because he knew that his parents were looking at him and waiting to hear what he had to say, he had said, "I guess I would," and Mr. and Mrs. Clarke had appeared to be satisfied with his answer. During the next few weeks he had helped with the preparations that were made for the coming of Hester. He and Mr. Clarke had cleared everything out from the loft and carried the boxes and barrels to the barn. Mrs. Clarke had scrubbed the floor and put a curtain up at the window. Mr. Clarke had made a bed and his wife had filled a mattress and a pillow, and all the time Ben had been angry and resentful that so much was being done for a girl whom no one had ever seen. Even Miss Foster at school had asked him about Hester.

"I expect you're all looking forward to her coming," the teacher had said. "We must all do what we can to help her settle down."

When Mr. Clarke had driven back from Halifax with Hester and Bethanne, Ben had felt a flash of anger when he saw the two girls sitting in the front of the buggy. In my place, he had thought, as he went inside the house to tell Mrs. Clarke and Mr. Gifford that his father had arrived. He was unaware that beneath the folds of their black cloaks the girls were trembling. When Hester had taken off her bonnet and revealed her cropped hair, nervous laughter had burst from him, but he had been ashamed when he saw the look of apprehension on her face, and after Hester had gone to bed, Mrs. Clarke had spoken to him about his behavior.

"We're all going to be shy with each other for a little while, Ben," she said. "Do all you can to help Hester feel at home."

"All right, Ma," he said, but when he came home from school the next day and had seen Hester wearing some of his clothes as calmly as if she had a right to use anything that belonged to him, he thought that she was already behaving as if she had always lived with them, and he wondered why his parents had taken in a strange girl from England who looked for all the world like a boy. As he saw the gentle way in which both his mother and father spoke to Hester, it seemed to him that they thought more of her than they did of him, and he began to watch her with a hard, cold feeling of resentment.

As Ben ran down the road, Hester knew that he had not wanted her to come to live with his parents in Silver Falls. She wondered if he had guessed how little there was in the bundle that she had brought from the asylum. She would have liked to run back to the house for the reassurance of Mrs. Clarke's kindness, but she felt that she could not tell her what Ben had said, and that she must not be late for school on her very first day. Clutching her lunch bundle, she hurried as quickly as she could past the entrance to

Pollitt's Spread and made her way down to the village, thinking, as Mr. Clarke had said, that it was easy to find one's way in Silver Falls. Other children were walking along the sidewalk to the school and she was glad that she was going to be in time.

The schoolhouse was a low, wooden building with three windows. In the yard the children of Silver Falls awaited the arrival of their teacher. In all there were twenty-five, their ages ranging from four to eleven. As Hester went into the yard, Ben and two other boys were playing a game of tag, and as he ran past her, although he said nothing, he was secretly glad that she had been able to find the schoolhouse. One of the bigger girls stared at Hester as she stood alone by the fence, but then a small boy who was chasing his friend suddenly tripped and fell down, and the girl ran to help him up and began to brush the dust from his clothes. Then a woman wearing a green bonnet and shawl and a plaid dress and carrying a basket in which there was a posy of ferns and flowers came into the yard, and when she called out, "Good morning, boys and girls," Hester thought that she must be the teacher.

"Good morning, Miss Foster," the children said, and then Hester remembered that she was the young woman who had played the organ in church on Sunday afternoon. Miss Foster unlocked the schoolhouse door and the children began to follow her inside. Ben looked at Hester, and with a jerk of his head indicated that she should follow him. She hoped that he would take her to the teacher, but instead he put his cap on one of the row of wooden pegs and then went to his seat at the back of the room.

Hester stood uncertainly by the door, waiting for the teacher to speak to her, while the other girls hung up their bonnets, shawls, and cloaks. The schoolhouse was long and narrow and could be heated by an iron stove, which was surrounded by a tall screen. The girls sat on the right-hand side of the room, and the boys on the left. The teacher's desk was set on a low platform, and on the wall behind it was a long blackboard. At the corner of the platform there was a pail of water. Still wearing her green bonnet and shawl, Miss Foster took a dipper from the wall and filled a brown jar with water from the pail and then began to arrange her posy of ferns and flowers.

Suddenly she looked up and saw Hester standing by the door. "It's Hester Fielding, isn't it?" she said.

"Yes, ma'am," Hester said, wishing that her voice could be firm and steady.

"Come along in, then," said the teacher. "Hang your bonnet and cloak on one of the pegs." Then she looked at Ben. "Why didn't you bring Hester to me, Ben?" she said. "Leaving her just like that. You should have known better."

Ben said nothing, but his face was red as he looked down at his desk. Hester walked over to the row of pegs, conscious of the noise her shoes made on the scrubbed floorboards. She knew that everyone in the school was looking at her, and she dreaded the moment when she must take off her bonnet and the children would see her short hair.

Slowly she untied her cloak and hung it on the end peg. She looked down at her dress, seeing its rich brown color and the yellow trimming, and thinking of the kindness of Mrs. Clarke, she found the courage to untie the strings of her bonnet. She placed it on the peg and waited with her hands clenched for the ripple of laughter. But there was no sound of amusement from the class. The children just sat looking at her with a friendly curiosity in their eyes. Surprised, Hester looked at Miss Foster. Then she knew why no one had laughed.

The teacher had taken off her bonnet and shawl. Miss Foster's hair was cut short, like a boy's. She smiled at Hester. "Ready, then, Hester?" she asked.

"Yes, thank you, ma'am," said Hester, wondering why the teacher's hair was cropped short.

"You can sit at the back of the room next to Lottie Savin," said Miss Foster, and the big girl who had helped the little boy when he fell down in the yard grinned as Hester walked to the back of the schoolroom and sat next to her.

"That's a pretty dress," she whispered, and Hester smiled back.

"No talking," said Miss Foster. She opened a big black Bible and read a chapter from the New Testament, and then everyone stood up and said the Lord's Prayer. After Miss Foster had called out all the names, she asked Ben to give out the slates and chalk, and he went to get them from the cupboard at the back of the room.

Then Miss Foster wrote some numbers to be added up on the blackboard. There were twenty problems altogether, and she said that the older boys and girls were to see how many they could do, while she taught part of the alphabet to the very young children, who were sitting in the front row of desks. Hester worked at her additions carefully, anxious not to make any mistakes. Ben was the first in the class to fill both sides of his slate, and then he went up to Miss Foster's desk so that she could check his work.

"Ben's always first," Lottie whispered. Her brother Tom was next, and then she took her work to the teacher. Lottie was very pleased when she came back to her desk because she had only one addition wrong. Hester was just finishing her sixth problem when Miss Foster said, "Let me see how you are getting on, Hester," and so she took her slate and showed it to the teacher. Although two of the additions were wrong, Miss Foster seemed quite satisfied. When Hester went back to her seat she was aware that Ben was looking at her, and she thought that he had been listening to what Miss Foster had said about her work so that he could tell Mrs. Clarke. The next time that Miss Foster asked to see Hester's work, all her additions were correct.

"You're doing well on your first day," Miss Foster said, and Hester wondered if Ben would tell his mother that as well. When the teacher said, "Recess, boys and girls," everyone stopped working and went out into the yard.

"Come on," Lottie said to Hester and they went to the far end of the yard, where there was a log bench.

"You've come over from England, haven't you?" Lottie said as they sat down.

"Yes," said Hester. Beneath a bow of black ribbon Lottie's hair coiled like a spring.

"Ma and Pa came from Somerset," Lottie said, "but that was before any of us were born." She told Hester that she had two brothers, Tom and Jim. "That's Tom over there with Ben, and Jim's the youngest boy in the school," she said. She also had an elder sister, Rachel. "Aunt Min took sick and Rachel had to go into Millford to look after her and housekeep for Uncle Jack," said Lottie. "Will, her young man, has been busy clearing his acreage and now he's building a house so that it will be ready when he and Rachel can be married."

Hester was grateful to Lottie for her friendly conversation, and the recess passed very quickly. When they went back into the schoolhouse, Miss Foster gave them some more additions to do, and then she had the children read. There was only one book and it was passed to each child in turn.

No one went home at midday. When it was lunchtime, Miss Foster hung the dipper on the side of the pail of water on the platform and placed two tin mugs on one of the desks in the front row so that anyone who was thirsty could have a drink. Lunch was a simple meal for everyone. The children ate slices of bread and cheese or bread and butter. Miss Foster had brought her lunch wrapped in a white napkin and in a small basket, and the bread was of her own baking and the butter had been churned by her neighbor.

Hester enjoyed her lunch. Now that she knew that no one really minded about her hair, she thought that she would like coming to school. She glanced across to where Ben sat with Tom Savin. He was laughing at something that Tom had said, and she thought how like his father he was when he was not looking sullen and angry. She thought again of what he had said on the way to school.

After the lunch recess was over, Miss Foster placed a globe of the world on her desk and the children had a geography lesson. Then they learned a poem and a song, and after that Miss Foster read a story.

School ended at three o'clock, and most of the children would have work to do when they went home. In Silver Falls all the boys and girls did the afternoon milking as soon as they were old enough. After Miss Foster had read the home-going prayer, everyone hurried to the row of pegs for caps, bonnets, shawls, and cloaks. As Hester was putting on her cloak, Miss Foster said, "I'd like a word with you, Hester, before you go."

"Yes, Miss Foster," Hester said. Holding her bonnet she stood by the teacher's desk. Miss Foster looked kindly at her. "Well," she said, "your first day's over."

"Yes, ma'am," said Hester. The day had gone far better than she had hoped.

"I expect that you'll soon settle down with Mr. and Mrs. Clarke," said Miss Foster, "and with Ben and Davy."

"Yes, ma'am," said Hester again, thinking of all the care that Mrs. Clarke had taken to transform the plain gray uniform dress, but remembering, too, Ben's angry words.

Miss Foster touched her hair. "At the beginning of the year I was ill with a fever," she said, "and I had to have my hair cut off. The minister took my place here while I was away. I'm looking forward to the time when I can have long braids again. I expect you are, too. I wonder whose hair will grow more quickly—yours or mine?"

Hester felt unable to say that she had never been allowed to have her hair in braids. She was not even sure that Miss Foster knew anything about the Marcroft orphan asylum back in England, but in the morning, after Hester had taken off her bonnet, the teacher knew why she had stood so forlornly by the door of the schoolhouse.

"Off you go, then," she said. "I must get things ready for tomorrow's lessons, and you mustn't keep Ben waiting."

"Thank you, ma'am," said Hester. She wondered why it was that a strange, aching feeling came into her throat when anyone was especially kind to her.

Miss Foster smiled as Hester went out into the yard. Then she placed a wooden cover on the water pail, and taking a broom from the corner of the room, she began to sweep the floor. When Hester closed the door of the schoolhouse she was not really surprised when she saw that Ben had not waited for her.

But Lottie was standing by the school gate with Jim. "All right?" asked Lottie.

"Yes, thank you," Hester said.

"I think that everyone likes Miss Foster," said Lottie. "She taught in a school at Halifax before she came here."

Jim took hold of Hester's hand and the three of them went along the sidewalk together. "You're honored," said Lottie. "Usually Jim wants to go chasing after Tom."

"Doesn't Tom ever wait for you?" said Hester.

"No," said Lottie comfortably. "Anyway, this week it's his turn to do the milking." When they came to the end of the sidewalk she said, "I'll see you tomorrow, then."

"Yes," said Hester. "Good-bye, Jim."

"Bye," said Jim.

As Hester began to walk back to the Clarkes' house she was glad that Lottie was prepared to be her friend. She thought of Bethanne and hoped that if she had gone to school that day, the teacher had been like Miss Foster and that there had been a girl as friendly as Lottie Savin. As she went by Pollitt's Spread, Mrs. Pollitt was taking a shirt from the clothesline. She waved as Hester passed, and Hester waved back, pleased that Mrs. Pollitt had recognized her. Remembering that Lottie had said that her brother Tom had not waited for her when school had ended because there would be the afternoon milking to do, she hoped that Mrs. Pollitt would not think it strange that Ben was not walking beside her. When she reached the Clarkes' house, she hesitated because the front door was shut. She went around to the back of the house, but the back door was also closed. At the orphanage none of the girls ever went into a room without first knocking on the door. Then they waited until they were given permission to enter. Hester hoped that perhaps Mrs. Clarke might come out and see her standing there, and so she waited for a few minutes. Then she knocked on the door and Mrs. Clarke came to open it.

"Hello, Hester," she said smiling. "Come on in."

"Thank you," Hester said.

"How did you get on at school today?" asked Mrs. Clarke as they went into the living room.

"All right, I think, Ma," said Hester, remembering the two additions that were wrong.

"That's good," said Mrs. Clarke. "Were the children friendly?"

"Oh, yes," Hester said. She said nothing about Ben, but she told Mrs. Clarke about Lottie Savin, and Mrs. Clarke seemed pleased. Hester took off her bonnet and cloak and hung them on her peg.

"You don't have to knock on either the front or the back door," said Mrs. Clarke. "Only people who come calling do that. Remember that this is your home, and we want you to feel easy and natural here, just as Ben does."

"Thank you, Ma," Hester said.

Mrs. Clarke had been busy. From a length of new material she had cut out a nightgown for Hester, and from an old blouse she had been able to find enough material for a sunbonnet. "Summer's not far away," she said, as she showed Hester the blue printed calico. "A sunbonnet will be useful when it's really warm," and although the material was faded because it had been washed so many times, to Hester, who in the past had worn the black uniform bonnet all year round, through summer and winter, it seemed as fashionable and elegant as anything worn by Lady Talbot.

"Thank you, Ma," she said, and Mrs. Clarke smiled. Hester had already started sewing the nightgown when

Ben came in from the cow shed after he had finished milking. She looked up and saw that he was staring at the material, and her hands trembled as she went on with her work.

When Mr. Clarke came home from the lumberyard, he asked her about her first day at school. She was still rather shy with him, but he looked at her kindly and she was able to tell him about Miss Foster and Lottie.

"You've always got Ben to keep an eye on you," said Mr. Clarke.

"Yes," said Hester, wondering what Ben was thinking as he sat next to his father. She looked at him over the rim of her mug, but he was staring down at his plate.

# Chapter 6

THE NEXT MORNING, although Ben and Hester set out for school together, as soon as they could no longer be seen from the house, Ben again ran off, leaving Hester to make her own way to the village. Sadly she watched him as he ran kicking a stone all the way along the rough road. Even though she realized that she could not yet expect a deep friendship to grow up between the two of them, she had at least hoped that Ben would have been prepared to accompany her to school.

But the second morning was quite different from the first. This time she knew that the other children were ready to accept her and that her short hair would pass unnoticed, and she walked briskly past the entrance to Pollitt's Spread. Already she was aware of a sense of freedom that the orphans at the asylum had never known. Here there were no high gray walls and long cold passages. Instead there was the open country with fields and trees. Everything seemed fresh in the sunlight and in spite of being alone, Hester felt her spirits rise and she knew that it was going to be a fine day. Lottie was already in the school yard and she came to meet Hester when she saw her on the sidewalk.

"Ben's been here a long time," said Lottie. "I thought that you might be sick or something."

"Ben can run a lot faster than I can," Hester said, hoping that Lottie would not guess what had happened.

"Ben's the best runner in school," said Lottie. "Anybody would have a hard time trying to keep up with him. In any case, school always starts soon enough, without anyone running all the way to get here early."

Miss Foster came into the yard and the children followed her into the schoolhouse. Caps, bonnets, shawls, and cloaks were hung on the pegs and then school began. After the Bible reading and the prayers, the older children went on with the arithmetic problems that Miss Foster had written on the blackboard before she went home on Monday evening. The small children in the front row of the class had a lesson in handwriting. After recess there was English grammar, followed by history until it was time for lunch. In the afternoon the boys had a drawing lesson, and there was sewing for the girls.

"Hand out the work, will you, Lottie, please?" said Miss Foster and Lottie went to the cupboard and took out a large black sewing bag. There were thirteen girls in the class and each of them, even Isobel McCann, the youngest pupil, was making an apron. Lottie went to each desk, handing the work to the girls, while Hester sat with her hands folded in her lap, suddenly conscious that she was a new girl and that not one of the pieces of material that Lottie was distributing belonged to her.

"Hester," said Miss Foster.

"Yes, ma'am," said Hester, and she hurried out to the front of the class.

"I cut out your apron last night," the teacher said, and from her basket she took out a piece of yellow-and-brown-checked material that was exactly the same as what the other girls had. A piece of paper on which was written Hester's name was pinned to the apron.

"Thank you, Miss Foster," Hester said.

"Have you done very much sewing?" asked Miss Foster.

"Yes, ma'am," Hester replied quietly.

"Good," said Miss Foster. "Here's a needle and thread. Be careful that you don't lose it."

Hester went back to her desk and began tacking the material.

"You're as quick as Miss Foster," said Lottie admiringly. She had been working on her own apron for several weeks, but she had not progressed very far because the teacher had said that the stitches were too big and uneven.

"No talking, Lottie," said Miss Foster, but from her desk she watched Hester for a little while longer before she stepped down from the platform to help Isobel, whose needle had become unthreaded.

Hester thought how strange it seemed to be using such brightly colored material for an apron, because at the asylum aprons had always been made of black calico, in accordance with the regulations. Before the lesson ended, she had finished all the tacking and had begun hemming the bib of the apron. She was pleased when Miss Foster praised the neatness of her sewing. The teacher also complimented Lottie on her work. Lottie had been impressed by Hester's skill, and she had tried very hard to make small, neat stitches.

After the home-going prayer had been said, Ben, Tom Savin, and Bill Masters, who were the three big boys in the school, ran off, and the other children went more slowly from the yard. Again, Jim, who was four years old, wanted to run after Tom, but Lottie held him firmly by the hand.

"You remember what Ma told you," said Lottie. "You're to come home with me. You can't expect to go chasing after Tom at your age."

"All right," said Jim. Hester looked at him, thinking of Davy in the cradle at home. When he was four years old, she would be fifteen. I wonder where I shall be then? she thought.

"Would you like to come home for a few minutes, Hester," said Lottie, "and meet Pa and Ma?"

Hester was not quite sure, because she felt rather shy at meeting new people and she thought that Mrs. Clarke would expect her to go straight home as soon as school had ended.

"Come on," said Lottie. "They'd like to meet you."

"All right," said Hester. "Thank you, Lottie."

The Savins owned the store in the main street of Silver Falls. Above the door there was a board on which were painted the words "Nathaniel Savin—General Storekeeper." Hester had never before in her entire life been inside a shop. On Sunday morning in England on their way to church, the girls looked at the bonnets in the shop window of Miss Ward, the milliner, and admired the glass and china in Johnson's Emporium.

There was also a toy shop in whose windows they could only glance fleetingly at wax-faced dolls, hoops, china tea sets and doll's-house furniture. Often they might have wished to have been able to look for a little while longer at a certain toy, but always either Miss Brown or Mrs. Dowding would be there, telling them to hurry or they would be late for church. On Sunday all the shops were shut, but even if they had been open, the girls could not have gone inside. They had no money, and everything that Lady Talbot considered to be necessary for the welfare of the orphans was to be found within the walls of the home.

When Hester went with Lottie and Jim into Mr. Savin's store, she thought that even if she had been in every shop in Marcroft, she would never have seen such a variety of merchandise gathered together under one roof. Every available inch of space seemed to be filled. The store was the only shop in Silver Falls, and since Millford was eight miles away, Mr. Savin tried to stock as many things as possible.

By the counter there were wooden bins lined with paper and containing tea, sugar, rice, and salt. Hams wrapped in linen hung from the ceiling beams and there was the smell of spices, leather, and new material. On a large table there were piles of plates and dishes, and rows of mugs, pitchers, jugs, and basins, and boxes of knives, forks, and spoons. Arranged on shelves there were bread crocks, oil lamps, shoes, racket-shaped snowshoes, saucepans, milking pails, blankets, and lengths of dress material. There was also what Mr. Savin laughingly called "The Silver Falls Tailoring Establishment," which was a long wooden rack from which hung jackets and trousers for men and boys. In a big glass jar on the counter there were long twisted sticks of candy, which were eyed hopefully by Jim.

Mr. Savin was adding up figures in a ledger, but he looked up as soon as he heard the sound of the door being opened. He was a short, gray-haired man, and he wore a white linen apron. "Hello," he said.

"It's only us, Pa," said Lottie. "I brought Hester in to see you and Ma."

"Pleased to meet you, Hester," said Mr. Savin.

"Thank you, sir," Hester said.

"We've heard a lot about you from Lottie," said Mr. Savin. "I hope you'll soon feel at home here in Silver Falls."

"Thank you," said Hester again, and then she followed Jim and Lottie past a barrel of vinegar and through the doorway that led into the Savins' living room. Mrs. Savin was busy ironing. She was taller than her husband and was wearing a dress of brown-and-black-striped material. A large basket heaped with clothes stood on the floor.

"This is Hester, Ma," said Lottie.

Mrs. Savin looked at Hester and smiled. "Hello, Hester," she said. She had the same friendly manner that Lottie possessed.

"Settling in all right?" asked Mrs. Savin.

"Yes, thank you, ma'am," said Hester.

"You'll soon get used to everybody," said Mrs. Savin. "Silver Falls is a friendly place to live in."

"Come on out the back," said Lottie. "I want to show you my garden."

Jim and the two girls went out through the living room and down the steps of the back porch. Most of the strip of garden was planted with vegetables, but there was a narrow patch in which violets and daisies were growing.

"Tom brought the plants home from the forest," Lottie

said, "and we made a border with stones from the river. What I'd really like is a rose bush—just like Miss Foster has in her garden. Still, this'll have to do for now."

Hester admired the flowers and the border of stones.

"I expect the Clarkes would let you have your own garden, too, if you asked them," Lottie said kindly.

Hester smiled, but she thought that Mr. and Mrs. Clarke had given her so much already. If she asked especially for something, they might think that she was discontented and ungrateful. At the end of the garden there was a barn which Mr. Savin used as a stock room. There was also a cow shed, where Tom was doing the afternoon milking. He looked up and grinned at Jim, Lottie, and Hester as they stood by the door.

"Tom and I take turns to do the milking," said Lottie. "It's my turn next week. Can you milk, Hester?"

"No," said Hester, looking at Tom as he sat on a stool with his head against the flank of a large cow.

"You'll soon learn," said Lottie.

When Tom had finished milking the cow, Hester said that she thought it was time that she went home.

"All right," said Lottie. "And I guess Ma will be waiting for me to help her with the ironing."

Hester said good-bye to Jim and Tom, and then she and Lottie walked back to the house. Although Mrs. Savin was still busy ironing, there was a large pile of clothes in the basket. She looked up from her work and smiled when the girls went into the living room.

"Hester's just going, Ma," said Lottie.

"Thank you very much, Mrs. Savin," Hester said. "Good afternoon."

"Good-bye, Hester," said Mrs. Savin.

When Hester and Lottie went into the store, Mr. Savin was serving a customer, so the girls walked quietly out onto the sidewalk.

"See you tomorrow," said Hester.

"Yes," said Lottie. Hester walked to the end of the sidewalk and crossed over the road, and then Lottie went back into the living room to help her mother with the ironing.

"Hester seems a nice girl," said Mrs. Savin, as Lottie took off her bonnet and thought regretfully of the pile of clothes there was to be ironed before there was even a hint of supper. Mrs. Savin looked at the sturdy figure of her daughter, at her dark, glossy hair and the round, dimpled cheeks, and she thought of Hester's pale face beneath the black bonnet. She rested her hand on Lottie's hair and said, "I hope that you'll be good friends. Now come and give me a hand with the sheets."

The next afternoon when Hester arrived home from school Mrs. Clarke asked her to go to Pollitt's Spread.

"Mrs. Pollitt called this afternoon and stayed for half an hour, as she usually does on Wednesdays," she said. "When she'd gone I saw that her umbrella was on the back of the chair. Would you take it over to her, Hester, please? She's probably wondering where it is. She'd made several sick calls before coming here."

"Yes, Ma," said Hester. She was pleased to be asked to do something, but she was not really sure that she wanted to visit Mrs. Pollitt. The umbrella was very big and black, and the handle was shaped like the head of a goose. Hester set off for Pollitt's Spread, thinking that it was the second time in a week that she had gone visiting. She had liked Mrs. Savin immediately, because Lottie's mother was the kind of person with whom it was possible to feel at ease within a very few minutes of a first meeting. She thought of the morning at the Clarkes' house when Mrs. Pollitt had called to see if she had arrived safely from Halifax, and she remembered that the sharp way in which the visitor had spoken had made her feel even more shy and uncertain. As she went up the track to the farmhouse she knew that she would have to face Mrs. Pollitt without the protection of Mrs. Clarke, and she took a deep breath before knocking on the back door. When Mrs. Pollitt opened it, Hester thought that she looked very severe when she was not wearing a bonnet. Mrs. Pollitt's gray hair was drawn back tightly into a bun, and she was wearing a dark-brown apron over her black dress.

"Mrs. Clarke sent me over with your umbrella, ma'am," Hester said.

"I'm much obliged," said Mrs. Pollitt. "I've just been casting around in my mind as to where it could be. I was afraid that I'd left it at the Harpers' place, which is a tidy ride from here. Now that Abe Harper's on the mend at long last, I won't be going out there again until Monday."

Hester gave her the umbrella and was ready to go, but Mrs. Pollitt said, "There's no need for you to go back right away. Come in and sit for a spell. I was wondering when you would take it into your head to come visiting."

The living room was very similar to that of the Clarkes. There was a tall cupboard, two stools, a table and four chairs, and a dresser on which there were tin plates, dishes, and an oil lamp. On the top shelf of the dresser there were six cups and saucers. Mrs. Pollitt was obviously very busy. Two large iron saucepans were boiling on the stove, and there were about twenty bottles of varying sizes on the table. Hester wondered if perhaps she had come visiting at the wrong time.

"Sit yourself down," said Mrs. Pollitt as she settled herself into the rocking chair.

"Thank you, ma'am," said Hester. She sat on a stool, holding herself rather stiffly.

"Are you getting on all right at school?" asked Mrs. Pollitt.

"Yes, thank you, ma'am," said Hester.

"I've watched you go by," said Mrs. Pollitt. Hester hoped that she had not realized that Ben always ran on ahead, but Mrs. Pollitt had.

"You don't move as fast as Ben, do you?" she said. "Still, the air here in Silver Falls is the best in all the country, and you'll soon be as bright as a button, I expect." She glanced down at Hester's brown dress. "Take off that cloak and let me have a look at you," she said.

Hester obediently untied her cloak and stood before Mrs. Pollitt in her brown dress.

"That's what I call right handy looking," said Mrs. Pollitt. "Worth wearing a boy's clothes for, I dare say." She smiled and now that Hester knew that no one really minded about her cropped hair, she smiled back.

"Yes, ma'am," she said.

A rather strange smell was coming from the two saucepans on the stove.

"It's medicine time," explained Mrs. Pollitt. "I'm just making up a new mixture of cough medicine. I like it to stand for six months or so, then it can get to its full strength. Have you got a cough?"

"No, thank you, ma'am," said Hester quickly.

"There's no need to say it like that," said Mrs. Pollitt. "My medicine never hurt a living soul." She spoke quite sharply, and for a moment Hester thought that she was offended. "Leastways," said Mrs. Pollitt, "it's cured far more than it's killed." She laughed, and Hester smiled rather uncertainly, not entirely sure that Mrs. Pollitt was joking. Mrs. Pollitt suddenly stood up and went over to the dresser. She climbed on a chair and reached up for one of the cups and saucers on the top shelf.

"What do you think of that, then?" she said, as she put the cup and saucer on the table.

Hester went to the table and looked at the china, which was white with a pattern of ears of corn and scarlet poppies.

"It's pretty, ma'am," she said.

"There's six like that," said Mrs. Pollitt. "They came from England—all half dozen of them. They've come all that way without so much as a chip or crack on them. I've promised them to my two sons when they get wed. Three to George and three to Luke. I can't do fairer than that, can I? Not that either of them seem to be in much of a hurry to find a wife for themselves. I dare say that I make them too comfortable."

Hester looked again at the cup and saucer on the table. The cup seemed so fragile with its curled gilt handle, and she could not really imagine it being held in the large red hands of either George or Luke. Mrs. Pollitt took the cup and saucer from the table and replaced it on the top shelf of the dresser. Then she went to her workbasket and from a small leather case she took out a thimble.

"This is another of my treasures," she said. "It's made of real silver." She held it up and the thimble gleamed in the afternoon sunlight. "I'll let you hold it," she said graciously. "Silver's not like china. There's no fear of silver ever cracking. Here you are."

"Thank you, ma'am," said Hester. She held the thimble in the palm of her right hand, thinking that never before had she seen anything so valuable. Around the base of the thimble there was an engraved design of ivy leaves.

"That belonged to my mother," said Mrs. Pollitt, "and when she died—God rest her soul—because I was the eldest, it came to me. Before she was married, she was a maid to a fine young lady at a great house in Devonshire, and the thimble was a parting gift from her when my mother and father were wed. I think a lot of that thimble, and it doesn't go to anybody until I've put my needle into my pincushion for the very last time—which I hope won't be for a few more years yet."

"It's lovely," said Hester.

"I thought that you'd admire it," said Mrs. Pollitt. "Most people I've shown it to think it's real pretty, except, of course, folk who couldn't recognize an angel from Heaven, not even if he was to walk through the door this very minute."

She put the thimble back into its leather case and placed it on top of her workbasket. Then she lifted the lids of the iron saucepans, which were boiling on the stove, and stirred the bubbling contents. There was a nervous tickling in Hester's throat, and she was afraid that she might cough and so be obliged to take a spoonful of the medicine.

"What sort of a trip out here did you have?" asked Mrs. Pollitt. Hester told her about the train journey to Liverpool and the sea voyage in the *Annapolis Valley,* and Mrs. Pollitt pursed her lips.

"A steamship," she said. "You were lucky. It was mighty different when we set out twenty-five years ago. Times were bad in England, what with no work and prices being so high. It was twenty miles to the dock from where we were living, but I walked by my husband's side all the way, every step, so that we didn't have to spend good money for places on the stagecoach. Even when we went on board the ship, our troubles weren't over. You might say that was when they really began.

"Everything was overcrowded, and we were all crammed in—just like apples in a barrel. The captain was supposed to provide everybody with water and bread, and folk were expected to bring enough of their own victuals to last out the voyage. A lot of them didn't, and people went hungry. It was so close below deck. There never seemed to be any fresh air. We ran into a great storm and the ship was blown off course. I think we all thought that our end had come in that great tempest. People took sick and some of them died without ever seeing the new land. We all huddled together and prayed out loud—just as if we'd been in a church in England.

"When we came ashore at Halifax, it was pouring with rain and there was a bitter wind that seemed to go right through you, but we didn't care, because we were so glad to set foot on land after all those days at sea. My husband got his acreage and started clearing, and by the time George was born we had a two-bedroom house, a cattle shed, a couple of oxen, and a cow.

"There was another room built on the house the year Luke came along. We all worked hard, and then, just when the boys were able to do a man's work on the farm and things could have been a bit easier, my man died suddenly one evening in the garden. The doctor came out from Millford and said that he thought that he'd over-strained his heart." Mrs. Pollitt looked at the six cups and saucers on the top shelf of the dresser. "And the last time that I used those cups was on the day of his funeral, nearly seven years ago," she said.

She was silent for a moment as she thought of her husband who had worked so hard to make Pollitt's Spread the prosperous farm that it now was. Then she went to the dresser and from one of the shelves took down a plate on which there were some small squares of golden-brown candy. "Whenever I take anybody a bottle of my cough medicine," she said, "I always leave them a paper bag of candy to take the taste away. Even if you don't want to entrust yourself to the physic, you're welcome to try a piece of this."

"Thank you, ma'am," said Hester, thinking that in spite of Mrs. Pollitt's abrupt manner, she was not really so frightening as she at first appeared to be. The candy was hard and sweet and would last for a long time. The living room seemed to be filled with the smell of the cough medicine boiling in the two saucepans on the stove, and she wondered if the candy really would take away the taste of the medicine.

"Candy all right?" asked Mrs. Pollitt.

"Yes, thank you, ma'am," said Hester.

"It'll do you good if you can keep it down you," said Mrs. Pollitt. "Just like my physic."

Hester thought of the large bottle of cough medicine at the orphan asylum and she wondered if it was possible for Mrs. Pollitt's medicine to taste as unpleasantly as that always had. After the spoonful of mixture had been swallowed in the presence of the matron, there was no piece of candy to take away the bitterness, and the taste remained in the mouths of the girls for a long time afterward. Beth-anne had always had a cough, even in the summer.

"Where did you learn how to help people when they're sick, Mrs. Pollitt?" Hester said.

"Well, I knew about babies from my own two boys," said Mrs. Pollitt, "and as they grew up there were grazed knees to bind up, and thorns to be taken out of hands. Once there was a fever down in the village, and there wasn't hardly a house where there wasn't somebody who was mortally sick. I went there to do what I could—being no more than neighborly, really. Dr. Hall showed me how to do certain things, and that was that."

She laughed ruefully, but Hester realized that she enjoyed her work. Mrs. Pollitt opened the tall cupboard. "This is my special cupboard where I keep all my sick-visiting things," she said. On the top shelf there were two medical books and below there were some jars and bottles, and two neat piles of clean white linen that could be used as bandages.

"It doesn't seem much to keep everyone in Silver Falls fit and healthy, does it?" she said. "But it's better than nothing, and perhaps one day we'll have our own doctor, right here in Silver Falls—and maybe a hospital as well. There's no end to what people can do if they put their minds to it."

"I ought to be going back," said Hester, glancing at a clock on a small table.

"Yes," said Mrs. Pollitt. "Nothing ever got done while folk sat around with their hands folded in their laps. I hope you make yourself useful up at the Clarkes' house."

Hester thought rather guiltily that she had done very little so far, except some housework, sewing, and washing the dishes.

"In a new country," said Mrs. Pollitt, "I reckon there's a place for everybody, provided that they're prepared to work hard and don't expect manna from Heaven to drop down right in front of them. The main thing to do is to keep cheerful, even when times aren't so good, and to keep on working. It's no good complaining. You just have to set to. See that you remember that, young woman, and you'll not go far wrong."

"Yes, Mrs. Pollitt," Hester said, as she began to put on her cloak. "Thank you."

"There's nothing to thank me for," said Mrs. Pollitt. "Off you go. I'm obliged to you for the umbrella."

One of the saucepans suddenly boiled over with a great hissing and spluttering, and with an exclamation of impatience Mrs. Pollitt whirled around and hurried over to the stove.

"Good-bye, Mrs. Pollitt," said Hester quickly. She was afraid that laughter was going to bubble up inside her, just as the medicine had in the saucepan. She closed the door behind her and stepped out onto the back porch, glad to be in the fresh air again, after sitting in the living room and breathing the fumes of the cough medicine.

At the beginning of Hester's second full week in Silver Falls, when she and Ben were getting ready for school, Mrs. Clarke said, "I'll show you how to do the milking this afternoon when you come home, Hester."

"Yes, Ma," Hester said.

Mrs. Clarke smiled. "There's no call for you to go worrying," she said. "It's something that everybody has to learn—men and women, boys and girls."

Hester thought about the milking while she was at school and hoped that she would not do anything wrong.

Until the railway journey from Marcroft to Liverpool, she had never seen a cow. As the train passed through the open fields, herds of cattle had been grazing, but they were only small figures in the distance, glimpsed from the safety of the railway carriage. Maggie was rather large. Hester had realized that there was a great difference in the quality of the milk that came from the Clarkes' cow and that which had been in the tall pitchers at the asylum. At mealtimes, when Mrs. Clarke poured the milk into the mugs, it had no bluish tinge as it did at the orphanage, because she had no need to add water to it, as old Nan was obliged to do, in order to make it go farther. When school ended, Hester walked with Lottie and Jim to the end of the sidewalk and then hurried home to the Clarkes' house, while Ben, who was having a holiday from the afternoon milking, stayed down in the village with Tom.

"It's my turn to do the milking this week," Lottie had said. Ben still remained unfriendly, and spoke to Hester only when it was absolutely necessary.

"Was everything all right at school, Hester?" said Mrs. Clarke.

"Yes, thank you, Ma," Hester said. She took off her bonnet and cloak and hung them on her special peg, and then went over to the cradle and looked down at Davy. He smiled up at her, and she thought that it was easy to pretend that he was her own brother.

"Would you like to bring Maggie in from the field, Hester?" said Mrs. Clarke.

"Yes, Ma," said Hester.

She gently withdrew the forefinger of her left hand from Davy's grasp and walked across the yard to the small field. Maggie knew that it was milking time and she was already standing by the fence. Hester thought that there was a surprised look in Maggie's big brown eyes when she saw that it was not Ben who was coming to open the gate. For a moment she wondered if Maggie would refuse to come, but as soon as the gate was opened, Maggie began to amble toward the cow shed. Hester ran on ahead to open the door, and then the cow went inside and placidly began to eat the hay in the feed trough. Hester's fingers trembled as she slipped the halter around Maggie's neck and tied the strip of leather to the stall. She stood looking at the cow for a moment and then she went back to the house to tell Mrs. Clarke that everything was ready.

Mrs. Clarke was wearing a white mobcap and was tying an apron around her waist when Hester went into the living room. There was another cap and apron for Hester, and as she put them on she wished that she could feel as calm as Mrs. Clarke appeared to be. Ben's mother said how important it was that when one was handling milk, everything was clean. They went into her bedroom and washed their hands in the green-and-white basin, and then Mrs. Clarke poured some warm water into a small pail.

In the cow shed she washed the udders of the cow and then asked Hester to get the big milking pail that had been turned upside down to dry on the back porch. When Hester came back into the cow shed, Mrs. Clarke said, "Right, then, sit close to Maggie's side," and so Hester sat down on the milking stool with her forehead against Maggie's broad flank.

"Reach down and press," said Mrs. Clarke, and very gently Hester did as she was told, aware of the warm, soft flank of Maggie against her face. For a moment she wondered what would happen if the cow suddenly moved, but after a little while warm milk began to run into the pail.

"Well done, Hester," said Mrs. Clarke. Hester's face

was hot and flushed, but she went on milking and Maggie stood calmly eating the hay in the feed trough.

"There you are," said Mrs. Clarke, when she had made sure that the last drop of milk had been pressed into the pail. "I told you this morning that there was nothing to worry about."

She was pleased with the calm, steady way in which Hester had set about her new task. Hester looked at the milk in the pail with a feeling of pride and relief. More than anything, she wanted always to be able to please Mrs. Clarke. The warm milk was taken to the back porch and poured into two large pitchers and then set to cool in the washtub of water. While Mrs. Clarke scoured out the milking pail, Hester took Maggie back to the field. As she shut the gate, Hester said, "Thank you, Maggie," and it seemed to her that Maggie swished her tail in a gracious acknowledgment.

"How did the milking go?" asked Mr. Clarke when everyone was at supper in the living room.

"Hester did very well," said his wife.

Hester knew that her face was red. "Maggie did well, too," she said modestly. Both Mr. and Mrs. Clarke laughed, but Ben went on eating his supper and did not seem at all pleased.

# Chapter 7

$A$S SPRING TURNED into summer, Hester went on learning. She had made good progress with her milking lessons and was now able to follow Maggie into the cow shed without a feeling of apprehension. Hester and Ben shared the afternoon milking, each taking a turn for a week at a time, and although it was very pleasant to be able to stay talking with Lottie and Jim for a few moments on the sidewalk after school had ended, Hester always felt a thrill of importance when it was her turn to milk Maggie. She would put on her bonnet and shawl and hurry out from the schoolhouse, knowing that the cow would be waiting by the gate in the small field.

Every Saturday morning Mrs. Clarke made enough butter for the coming week. Cream was taken from the milk and put into the butter churn, and then the handle was turned until the butter came. After it had been washed in cold water, a small amount of salt was added before it was patted into shape.

On two Saturday mornings, in addition to watching everything that Mrs. Clarke did, Hester was allowed to prepare the salt. She took some from the jar on the shelf in the pantry and dried it in a metal dish on the stove. Then she put the dish on the table, and using the end of Mrs. Clarke's rolling pin, crushed the coarse crystals into a fine powder, ready for Mrs. Clarke to use. Ben's mother said how important it was that all the utensils were scalded with boiling water. When all the scouring was done, the churn, the dishes, skimmers, and dippers were set out on the front porch to dry in the open air.

The first time Hester was allowed to turn the handle of the churn her arm ached and she was out of breath, but Mrs. Clarke was pleased when she looked inside and saw the yellow butter. "You're going to be a good dairywoman, I can see that," she said encouragingly, and Hester forgot about her face being red and her arm aching.

She was also getting cooking lessons. She knew how to boil potatoes and was soon able to make the pastry for the Sunday pie. On Saturday afternoon she helped with the breadmaking.

Each evening except on Sunday, after Hester had sung Davy to sleep, she was busy with her sewing. She had made the nightgown, the sunbonnet, and an apron, and Mrs. Clarke had made her a skirt and a black-and-white-striped blouse. When all the clothes were made, Hester began to make a patchwork quilt for her bed in the loft, using the small pieces of material in Mrs. Clarke's ragbag. Everyone was busy. As soon as the evening meal was over, Mr. Clarke worked in the barn or out on the land, and

Ben went with him, learning everything his father could teach him.

Sometimes when Hester sat with her sewing, she looked across at Mrs. Clarke as she knitted socks or patched a pair of Ben's trousers. At Marcroft she had rarely thought about her own mother, but when Bethanne came to the home she had spoken of her parents and of the things that she could remember, and then Hester had begun to wonder what her own parents had been like. Since coming to live in Silver Falls, she hoped that her mother had been just like Mrs. Clarke.

One morning while Hester and Ben were at breakfast, Mrs. Clarke went into her bedroom and then called out to them.

"Come and see," she said.

Hester waited until Ben had put down his spoon and had gone to the door, and then she followed him. When they looked into the bedroom, they knew why Mrs. Clarke was so pleased. Davy had caught hold of the sides of the cradle and was sitting up and looking around at everything in the room with a slightly surprised air.

"It's six months to the day that he was born," said Mrs. Clarke. "I remember that you were just the same, Ben. You sat up at six months and were walking before your first birthday."

Hester stood smiling at Davy and she was pleased when he smiled back. She wondered how old she had been when she had sat up for the very first time, and if there had been the same excitement and happiness as there was that morning in the Clarkes' house.

"It's the growing season," said Mrs. Clarke.

As Hester walked to school that morning she knew

what Mrs. Clarke meant. In the forest the birch trees and maples were in fresh green leaf, making a bold contrast against the dark firs. The grass was growing tall in the fields. Mrs. Clarke thought that Hester was blossoming, too. There was a delicate color in her face, and her hair was beginning to grow.

The grass in the big meadow was at last ready to be cut, and one evening after supper Mr. Clarke and Ben went out and began haymaking. After Hester had put Davy to bed, Mrs. Clarke said that she could go and watch. Hester looked at the wide expanse of the field, and as the grass and flowers swayed in the breeze, she thought that a field of mowing grass was like the sea, full of movement and ever-changing colors of green, brown, and silver. She remembered how she had stared down at the water, realizing that she was leaving England forever, as the *Annapolis Valley* sailed out from Liverpool.

Mr. Clarke was at one end of the field in the tangle of grass and wild flowers. He was using a scythe and as it moved in a rhythmic, curving motion, the silvery-headed grass and the tall daisies fell beneath the bright, sharp blade. In the middle of the field Ben was at work with a reaping hook. He looked up and saw Hester standing by the gate and then he turned back again and went on cutting the grass. Hester was able to find a few violets and she also picked a spray of the pale-pink blossom which Mrs. Clarke had told her was the flower of the cranberry.

"The berries are ripe about the end of September," she said. "We use them for sauce and pies. Pa and Ben like cranberry sauce with a slice of cold meat."

Hester sat looking at Mr. Clarke and Ben as they moved across the field cutting the grass. She felt rather guilty watching other people work and not doing anything herself, and when she saw Mrs. Clarke coming with a pitcher and a tin mug, she went across to meet her.

"Haymaking is thirsty work," said Mrs. Clarke. "They'll both be glad of a drink."

Hester held the mug while Mrs. Clarke poured the water into it.

"That's for Pa, then," she said.

"Yes, Ma," said Hester, and she walked across the freshly cut grass to where Mr. Clarke was working.

"Thank you, Hester," he said. He wiped the perspiration from his forehead with his hand, and then drank from the mug. Although he had rolled up his sleeves and the front of his gray flannel shirt was open all the way down the front, his face was red and he looked very hot.

"I needed that," he said, smiling, as he gave the empty mug back to Hester.

"Do you want any more, Pa?" said Hester, just as Mrs. Clarke always asked at mealtimes.

"No, thank you," said Mr. Clarke. "Not for a while yet. That'll set me up for the time being." He looked up at the sky. "It's a grand evening," he said. He went on using the scythe, and Hester walked back to where Mrs. Clarke was standing by the fence. She held the mug while it was again filled with water, and for a moment she hoped that Mrs. Clarke would say that she would take the drink out to Ben, but instead she said, "That's for Ben, then, Hester," and so Hester went across the field to where Ben was.

Whenever they were by themselves in the living room, she kept her eyes on the work she was doing, whether it was sewing or washing the dishes. Once she had dropped one of the tin plates, and she knew that her face flamed with embarrassment as she bent down to pick it up conscious of the fact that Ben was watching her, although he was pretending to be occupied with cleaning all the knives from the box of cutlery.

There was always a silence between them, and although she was ready to be friendly and to respond to what he had to say, she knew that she must wait for Ben to be the first to speak. She walked to school by herself quite cheerfully, but when Lottie spoke of her brother Tom, of the things he said and did, Hester wondered if there would ever come a time when there would be a happy, easy relationship between Ben and her, just as there was between Tom and Lottie. Sometimes she thought that perhaps she was expecting too much, because however hard she pretended, she knew that Ben and Davy would never be her real brothers. They never could be.

Although she had not known her mother and father, at the orphan asylum in Marcroft there had been the companionship of the other girls through the years, and then, when she was eight, Bethanne had come and had been her special friend, and the friendship had lightened the long afternoons spent scrubbing, sewing, washing, and ironing.

Since coming to live in Silver Falls, Hester knew what it was to be a member of a family, with her own bedroom up in the loft and her own set of daily tasks. She was beginning to think of the Clarkes as her parents, just as Mrs. Clarke had told her on the first evening, and it was easy to pretend that Davy was her brother. But Ben was always there to remind her, either with a glance or simply by not saying anything at all, that she was not a real member of the Clarke family. She knew that he did not really want her to call Mr. and Mrs. Clarke "Ma" and "Pa," as his mother had said. They were his parents and not hers.

Mrs. Clarke had filled the mug almost to the rim, but although the grass was quite slippery, Hester was able to reach Ben without spilling any of the water. He saw her coming and he carefully laid the reaping hook down on the cut grass.

"Thanks," he said gruffly, as Hester gave him the mug. She moved away and looked at the green swathes of grass, thinking how hard he had worked, using only the small reaping hook. She picked up a daisy that lay among the grass. She was not sure why she did, but she was able to look at it while waiting for Ben to finish the water.

"Thanks," he said again, when he handed her the mug.

"You're welcome," Hester said softly, and Ben looked at her and then began to cut the grass again. Hester wished then that she had not said anything to Ben, but when anyone thanked Mrs. Clarke for something that she had done for them, she always smiled and said, "You're welcome." Hester knew that Ben, as the elder son of the Clarke household, had a far better right to water from his father's well in the front garden than she had.

"All right?" asked Mrs. Clarke when Hester came back to her.

"Yes, thank you, Ma," she said. When they went back into the house, Mrs. Clarke looked into the bedroom and smiled when she saw that Davy was fast asleep in the cradle. Hester arranged the violets, the spray of cranberry blossom, and the daisy in the blue vase, and placed it on the dresser. Before coming to live in Silver Falls, she had never been able to walk in the fields and to find wild flowers.

"How nice they look," said Mrs. Clarke. "You've a way with flowers, Hester."

So have you, Ma, Hester thought, remembering those that had been on the shelf in the loft on her first day in Silver Falls.

Mrs. Clarke took out her workbasket and went on with her mending and Hester brought her patchwork down from the loft. They sat together working quietly until Ben came in at half past eight.

"Can I have a towel, please, Ma?" he said. "We're going to cool off in the river."

"Don't stay in too long," said Mrs. Clarke. She went to the cupboard and gave him an old towel.

"All right, Ma," said Ben, and as he ran off, Hester wondered if she would ever be able to learn to swim.

On Wednesday evening, while Ben and Mr. Clarke were cutting the grass in the second half of the big field Mrs. Clarke and Hester put on their sunbonnets and went out to toss the grass that had been cut two days earlier.

"We want to get it dried as quickly as possible," said Mrs. Clarke. She showed Hester how to use a pitchfork so that the drying grass stood in furrowed peaks. "It's quite easy," she said.

"Yes, Ma," said Hester. She went to the far end of the field and began tossing the grass, surprised to find that although it was dry on top, underneath it was still damp from the morning dew. She looked across to where Mrs. Clarke in her gray sunbonnet and faded print dress was working and then at Mr. Clarke and Ben as they cut the tall, shimmering grass. She glanced back to the house where Davy was asleep in his cradle, and she felt a great sense of belonging, glad that Mr. and Mrs. Clarke trusted her to take her share in the work. She enjoyed using the pitchfork to lift the grass, even though sometimes the pollen made her sneeze.

"We've done well," said Mrs. Clarke at the end of the evening. The crop seemed much larger now that it no longer lay flat on the ground. It would be shared between

Maggie and Blackie. Mrs. Clarke looked down at Hester and saw her red face beneath the frill of the sunbonnet.

"The sun's caught your face," she said, laughing.

"And yours, Ma," said Hester.

At Marcroft the work of the orphanage went on in the usual way, regardless of the seasons of the year. The only difference between the summer and winter had been that in the summer the rooms and long passages were less cold than they were in the winter.

When the haymaking began, Hester learned how important the weather was to the people who lived in Silver Falls. "Red at night, shepherd's delight," Mrs. Clarke said, and before undressing, Hester looked out from the window of the loft and was pleased when she saw the splendor of the sunset. Sometimes clouds were tipped with gold and the sky was washed with flame and silver. In the orphan asylum there had been so little color. Looking back, she thought that everything there had been gray, white, and black. In Silver Falls the colors of summer were everywhere, in the sky, in the fields, and in the forest. She saw how beautiful the gleam of sunlight on a river could be and how the sight of a flock of birds against the evening sky could bring a feeling of contentment.

During the days of the haymaking most of the children's faces were reddened by the sun. When school ended, there was no loitering in the yard, and none of the boys stayed to watch the blacksmith at the forge. All the children hurried home, and when the milking was done, they went out to the fields carrying pitchforks and long, wooden rakes. At lesson time everyone listened attentively to Miss Foster, and arithmetic and writing were carefully and painstakingly accomplished. No one wanted to stay behind after three o'clock and sit in a silent schoolhouse doing extra lessons while the work in the hayfields was waiting. Ben ran most of the way back home and he always arrived before Hester, who also hurried as quickly as she could. As soon as she had finished milking Maggie and had set the pitchers of milk to cool in the washtub, she put on her sunbonnet and went to work in the hayfield. When all the grass had dried, it was raked into great heaps, ready to be pitchforked up into the haycart. When Mr. Clarke came home in the evening, he lifted the hay into the wagon where Ben stood waiting to receive it, and then, when it was piled as high as it safely could be, Blackie pulled the cart back to the yard. While Mr. Clarke began to make the rick, Mrs. Clarke, Hester, and Ben went back to the field to bring in another cartload of hay.

"It's a good crop this year," said Mr. Clarke, when all the hay had been brought in from the field. Everyone smiled as they looked at the hayrick in the yard, all sharing in the sense of achievement which helped to lessen the discomfort of an aching back, stiff forearms, and blistered palms. The hay would be allowed to settle for a few weeks, and then it would be covered with straw.

It had been arranged that after the Clarkes' haymaking was finished, they would help with the hay at Pollitt's Spread, where there were several fields of grass to be cut. The next afternoon, as soon as school had ended, instead of going home, Ben went straight to Pollitt's Spread to work with George and Luke. When Hester had finished the afternoon milking, she also went to the farmhouse. Mrs. Pollitt was just coming across the yard from the cow shed.

"Hello, Hester," she said. "Have you come to give us a helping hand, then?"

"Yes, please, ma'am," said Hester, hoping that whatever she was told to do, she would be able to do to Mrs. Pollitt's satisfaction. She went with her to one of the fields and they began raking the hay. In the next field George was standing in the cart, ready to accept the hay from Luke and Ben.

Mrs. Pollitt worked quickly. She raked the hay vigorously and seemed untroubled by the heat. The sunbonnet she wore was much larger than that owned by Mrs. Clarke. Mrs. Pollitt's red face glowed beneath the broad brim of the pink printed calico and the pleated curtain that shielded her neck from the sun fell almost to her waist. Hester worked as quickly as she could, hoping that she would be able to keep up with Mrs. Pollitt as they moved across the field.

"There's no need to go knocking yourself out," said Mrs. Pollitt, who, in spite of the sheltering sunbonnet, was able to observe how speedily Hester was raking the hay. "Stop and rest for a spell when you want to."

They raked the hay into heaps ready for George, Luke, and Ben, and when there was only a small amount of raking to be done, Mrs. Pollitt said, "I'll go and start supper now. I'll ring the hand bell when it's ready, so mind that you listen for it."

"Yes, Mrs. Pollitt," said Hester. She turned back again to her work, thinking how much she would enjoy a drink of water. The sun was very hot and the sky was quite blue, without even the smallest cloud. Once she looked across to the edge of the forest, where she knew it would be cool beneath the branches of the trees.

When supper was ready, Mrs. Pollitt went out into the yard and rang the hand bell, and its harsh jangling sound made Hester remember the cold, early mornings in the dormitory at the orphan asylum, when Miss Fitch came in to tell everyone that it was time to get up. Hester wondered if Ben, George, and Luke in the next field had heard the bell, but when she looked around she could see that the big cart was coming through the gateway. Ben was sitting in front with the Pollitt brothers, who were wearing old straw hats. They were laughing at a remark he had made, and Hester thought that perhaps he might have said something about her.

"Supper's up," said George, as the cart, piled with hay, came near to where Hester was standing. "We don't want to keep Ma waiting. Up you get, Hester." He jumped down and lifted her up into his seat next to Ben, and then he walked by the side of the cart. "It looks as if you've been busy," he said, glancing at the raked hay, which was now all heaped, ready for the cart. "We shall have to work a bit faster to keep up with you, I can see."

He looked at Hester and grinned, and Hester smiled back, glad that he was pleased. Ben looked at her and then went on talking to Luke, and Hester felt that he was wishing that she were not there, and that George were sitting up in the seat next to him. She suddenly felt rather nervous at the prospect of having a meal in the living room at Pollitt's Spread, and when they reached the yard she thought that she would much prefer to go home to Mrs. Clarke. But in Silver Falls it was the custom to be given supper in return for helping a neighbor with the hay-making. Mr. Clarke had come to Pollitt's Spread as soon as he had finished work in the lumberyard, and Hester was glad that he was there on the back porch with Mrs. Pollitt, who was still holding the hand bell.

"I waited until I saw your pa coming up the track before I rang the bell," she said. "Come on in, everybody." They all followed her into the living room of the farm-house.

"You sit next to me, Hester," said Mrs. Pollitt, "and you sit next to her, Mr. Clarke, and Ben can be between George and Luke." George said grace, and then Mrs. Pollitt said, "Right. Everyone sit down and get started."

For supper there were boiled potatoes, pickles, and cold meat.

Ben and Hester had milk to drink, and for the grown-ups there was a pitcher of cider.

"Fine-tasting cider, Mrs. Pollitt," said Mr. Clarke appreciatively.

"It was a good crop of apples last year," said Mrs. Pollitt. "One of the best we've had for some time now."

As Hester ate her supper she thought that last year she had been in England, with no possibility of ever leaving the orphanage until a place in service had been found for her. Yet here she was, eating supper with the Pollitts, Ben, and Mr. Clarke, in a room that was so different from any that had been in the asylum. The food was different, too, she thought. Mrs. Pollitt had given everyone generous helpings, and there was bread and cheese to end the meal.

"Let's have another drop of cider, Ma, please," said Luke. "Then we must be making a start."

"We don't want to get too comfortable," said Mr. Clarke, laughing, but Mrs. Pollitt again filled the mugs with cider from the pitcher. Hester had never seen cider before, and as she looked at its tawny, golden color, she wondered if she would like its taste. She helped Mrs. Pollitt with the dishes while Ben and his father went back to the field with George and Luke.

"Did you enjoy your supper, young woman?" asked Mrs. Pollitt.

"Yes, thank you, ma'am," said Hester.

"I like to see people eat hearty," Mrs. Pollitt said, as

she looked at the empty potato dish. "There's never likely to be very much wrong with anybody who can eat well."

There had been many occasions in her life, both in England and in Silver Falls, when she had been able to place only a frugal meal of bread and potatoes on the table.

"The Clarkes have always been good neighbors to us," she said, as Hester carefully dried the plates and mugs. "And as soon as Ben was old enough, he came to help with the haymaking and the harvesting as well."

Hester, Mr. Clarke, and Ben worked at Pollitt's Spread until all the hay had been brought in from the fields. Each evening Mrs. Pollitt prepared a large supper and gave a nod of satisfaction when she saw how quickly the food disappeared from the plates. A large hayrick was built in the farmyard, and a smaller one in the corner of the first field, where it would be sheltered by two trees.

"Can we rely on you to come and thatch the ricks in a few weeks, Mr. Clarke?" asked Mrs. Pollitt. "There's plenty of straw left in the barn."

"I'll be pleased to," said Mr. Clarke.

"He's better at thatching than the boys are," Mrs. Pollitt said to Hester, and Hester felt a thrill of pride.

"Right, then," said Mrs. Pollitt, looking at George and Luke. "It's time to settle up."

For his help in the haymaking, George and Luke gave Mr. Clarke a sack of flour.

"I'm much obliged," said Mr. Clarke.

"It's no more than it should be," said Mrs. Pollitt. "Besides, you've an extra mouth to feed now."

She spoke in her usual abrupt manner, but Hester knew that Mrs. Pollitt was referring to her, and although she clenched her hands, her face reddened as she looked down at her shoes. She wondered if Ben thought of her in that way—as someone to be fed and clothed from the little that his parents had to spare. It seemed to her that all her life she had been a burden to someone, first of all to the taxpayers of Marcroft, and now to Mr. and Mrs. Clarke. For a moment she wished that she was grown up, dependent on no one for anything, and being able to work for her living and earn her own keep. She glanced at Mr. Clarke, but he had seen the color rise in her face, and from his reassuring smile she knew that there had been no intended malice in what Mrs. Pollitt had said.

The settling up also included something for the two young helpers. Ben received a leather belt and a bag of Mrs. Pollitt's candy.

"Thank you, Mrs. Pollitt," said Ben, fingering the big clasp on the belt.

"That's all right," said Mrs. Pollitt, but she was glad that he was pleased with the gift.

For Hester there was a basket with six brown eggs in it, a bag of candy, and some pieces of material for her patchwork.

"Thank you, Mrs. Pollitt," said Hester.

"You're welcome," replied Mrs. Pollitt. "There's no taste to nothing, and you've all worked hard. Let me have that basket back in a day or two, and when the patchwork quilt is finished at long last, I hope that you'll ask me to step inside to see it."

"Yes, I will," said Hester, thinking that she would have to ask Mrs. Clarke first of all. One of the pieces of material that Mrs. Pollitt had given to her was bright red, and she thought that it would enliven some of the dark colors in the patchwork, but the gift that pleased her most of all was the cluster of eggs in the little basket. She would be able to give them to Mrs. Clarke with the thought that everyone could share in something that she alone had earned. For the first time in her life, instead of receiving the charity of others, she had something to give.

Mr. Clarke pushed the sack of flour home in a wheelbarrow and Hester and Ben, each eating a piece of Mrs. Pollitt's candy, walked on either side of him. During the haymaking at Pollitt's Spread, Mrs. Clarke had thought how quiet it seemed at home. It was almost as if it had been more than eleven years ago, when, instead of Davy, Ben had been the baby in the cradle. She came to the window as Mr. Clarke, Ben, and Hester walked up the path. In spite of the hardships, the years in Silver Falls had been good, and Mrs. Clarke looked with eyes of love at the broad figure of her husband. She opened the door and stood on the front porch, and Ben ran to show her his new belt and to offer her a piece of candy. He tried the belt on and found that some more holes needed to be made in the leather, so he hurried indoors to find a meat skewer. Then Hester went to Mrs. Clarke and gave her the basket of eggs and the bag of candy.

"Mrs. Pollitt sent these, Ma," she said, and she felt very happy when she saw how pleased Mrs. Clarke looked.

"We'll each have a fried egg for breakfast on Sunday," Mrs. Clarke said. She went down the steps to see the sack of flour, and while Mr. Clarke took the wheelbarrow around to the barn, she and Hester went indoors and Hester showed her the material for the patchwork. Mrs. Clarke admired everything. She liked the piece of red cloth especially.

"It's lovely," she said. "It's almost the color of a holly berry. I wonder where Mrs. Pollitt got that from. I haven't seen anything as pretty as that for many a day."

Hester would have to work very hard at the patchwork

in order to make enough for a quilt to cover her bed in the loft, but she knew that when it was at last finished, the pieces of red would always remind her of haymaking in Silver Falls, and of the time when she received her first wages of patchwork material, a bag of candy, and six brown eggs.

# Chapter 8

"*I*'M GOING into the forest tonight," said Mr. Clarke one evening when everyone was at supper in the living room. "Like to come, Ben?"

"Yes, please, Pa," said Ben.

"I need some more staking," said Mr. Clarke. "Would you like to come as well, Hester?"

Hester smiled and looked at Mrs. Clarke, thinking that she had not yet sung the lullaby to Davy, and that there would be the dishwashing to do.

"That'll be all right, Hester," Mrs. Clarke said. "You can go with Pa and Ben."

"Thank you, Ma," Hester said. She wondered what Ben was thinking. She looked across the table to where he was sitting, but he went on eating his supper. Instinctively she knew that he would have preferred to go off alone with his father, but ever since her first day in Silver Falls, she had hoped that she would be able to go into the forest.

As soon as supper was over, Mr. Clarke and Ben went out to the barn. Hester began to clear the table, but Mrs. Clarke said, "I'll see to the dishes, Hester. Pa'll be ready in a minute or two, so get your sunbonnet and off you go."

Hester put on her sunbonnet and went out to the yard. Ben and his father were coming from the barn. Mr. Clarke was pushing a wheelbarrow in which there was a large ax and a coil of rope.

"Ready, then, Hester?" he said.

"Yes, please," Hester said, and Mr. Clarke gave her an encouraging smile, thinking of their first meeting in the parlor of the minister's house in Halifax. He remembered how she had stood trembling, and the curtsy she had made when Miss Hayward had told her who the big dark-bearded figure was.

"It was just as if I'd been one of the gentry back in England," he told Mrs. Clarke, and she knew that he had been touched by Hester's shy, awkward gesture of humility. He had seen the many ways in which Hester helped his wife in the house, with the butter making, the washing, ironing, and sewing; and he was aware, too, of the love which she gave to his baby son. Although he realized that there was an uneasiness in the relationship between Ben and Hester, he thought that this was due to the fact that Ben had been the only child in the house for a long time before Davy was born. Ben had never grown up with brothers and sisters, as his mother and father had. Mr. Clarke knew that Ben and Tom Savin were good friends and that Lottie and Hester were friendly, too, and he hoped that in time Ben would begin to think of Hester as his own sister. Neither Mr. Clarke nor his wife knew that Ben always ran on ahead to the village, and that Hester had been left to make her own solitary journey on her very first day at school, because Hester felt that she could never tell anyone at home about what Ben did. Only Mrs. Pollitt knew, and she had not thought that there was anything unfriendly in Ben's action.

Mr. Clarke looked at Hester's sun-warmed face beneath the blue-and-white sunbonnet, and he thought again of their first meeting in Mr. Weston's house, remembering her pale face framed in the black bonnet. Already she seemed a different girl.

Mr. Clarke's mother had been a widow, but she was able to pay the rent of her cottage and to clothe and feed three children by taking in washing and sewing. She had also gone out scrubbing, doing anything to keep herself and her two sons and daughter free from the shadow of the workhouse. And then, when her daughter was settled in good service and her two sons were able to provide for her, Mrs. Clarke had died. But her children never forgot the sacrifices she had made, her brave spirit and her determination that they should stay together as a family and never have to make the slow, sad journey to the tall gray building situated on the outskirts of the town.

In England Mr. Clarke had worked on a farm, but after six years the farm was sold. The farmhouse and outbuildings were pulled down so that a gentleman's country residence could be built. Mr. Clarke was unable to obtain work, and it was then that he began to think of emigrating to Nova Scotia. When he spoke of his plan to his sweetheart, she agreed to go with him.

In Nova Scotia the Clarkes worked hard and they had prospered, but the life of a settler would never be easy. The land must always be tilled and sown, nothing could be wasted, and small luxuries were very few. Mr. Clarke and his wife had first heard of the work of the children's welfare agency from Mr. Anderson, and after careful thought they had decided to make an offer of a home to an orphan girl in England, wanting someone else to share in what they had achieved through the years of hard work.

When Hester went with Mr. Clarke and Ben through the fields she looked at the forest, which stretched as far as anyone could see, with fir, spruce, beech, hemlock, oak, and birch all crowding together. When they went over the log bridge a sudden whirring sound made her jump, and then a bird flew out from the trees, alarmed at the approach of human beings. Mr. Clarke and Ben walked steadily on, as if nothing strange had happened, but Hester wondered if Mr. Clarke had seen the involuntary movement of her shoulders.

Mr. Clarke left the wheelbarrow at the edge of the forest. He swung the ax up onto his shoulder and Ben carried the coil of rope. Inside the forest the air was cool beneath the great height of the trees, and the light of the summer evening was dimmed by the spreading branches. Thickets of bracken, waving mysteriously, almost smothered the trailing brambles and low-growing bushes. Ben led the way, with Hester following, and then, last of all, went Mr. Clarke. At first it seemed to Hester that the woods were quite silent, the only sounds being those that were made when anyone stepped on a dried twig, but as they went through the waist-high bracken, there were rustlings and quick movements in the undergrowth as the forest creatures became aware of their presence. She felt as if many eyes were watching her, and she thought of all the birds that must be perched in the branches high above, looking down on them as they went farther into the forest. Often the ground dipped into a sudden hollow, and her steps quickened so that she was nearly running. Sometimes it rose quite steeply, and she scrambled up behind Ben, almost out of breath. When they came to a clearing, Mr. Clarke went up to a tree and inspected its branches.

"This'll do, Ben," he said.

He laid the ax down on the ground and took off his jacket. He rolled up the sleeves of his shirt and then began to cut down the staking. As he worked, Hester admired the ease with which he handled the gleaming ax, until Ben said, "You may as well look for some kindling."

There was a certain reproof in the curt way in which he had spoken, as if he were angry that she had been wasting time.

"Yes, Ben," she said, and then she began to search among the undergrowth for the dried sticks. She looked back once and could no longer see either Ben or his father, but she was able to hear the sound of the ax as Mr. Clarke went on cutting his staking. She wondered what it would be like to be alone in the forest, especially at nighttime, and she thought that the sharp, attacking sound was also strangely reassuring.

She could hear the murmur of running water and she came to a bank and looked down at a shallow stream which flowed swiftly over its bed of gravel, twisting itself around large stones and sunken tree roots as if it were determined that nothing should prevent it from joining the river. Hester dropped a small piece of kindling into the water, and as it floated away she hoped that it would reach the village and be carried right over the waterfall. Again she had the feeling that she was being watched. She looked over at the other bank of the stream and she saw that a beaver was looking unblinkingly at her. She stood quite still, with a half-smile on her face, until a rustling noise behind her frightened the beaver and it scuttled away into the undergrowth. Hester turned and Ben was there with an armful of kindling, staring contemptuously at the few pieces of firewood that she had collected. For a moment she thought that she would tell him about the beaver, but she was afraid that he would think she was trying to find an excuse for not having found very much kindling, so she said nothing and waited for him to speak.

"You may as well take this load back to where Pa is," Ben said, "and I'll go on looking for a bit more. You don't seem to be much good at finding any."

Hester held out her arms and Ben gave her all the firewood which he had found and then she began to walk back to where Mr. Clarke was cutting the stakes. She wondered if Ben would tell his father that instead of looking for firewood, as she had been told to do, she had just been standing by the stream. When she reached the clearing, Mr. Clarke had already cut several stakes and was resting for a moment before going on to cut some more. He looked up as Hester came out from the bracken with the pile of kindling.

"You've done well, Hester," he said.

"Ben found nearly all of it," she said quickly, hoping that he would not ask her how many pieces were hers. She knew that she would feel ashamed to say that she had found only four small sticks. She placed the pile of kindling on the ground and then went back again into the undergrowth, searching anxiously for some more firewood, determined not to be frightened by any of the rustlings and twitterings in the bushes, and hoping to make up for the time that she had wasted. She went farther into the forest, carefully searching for pieces of wood until she had a pile of kindling in her arms.

It was only when she turned to go back that she realized

that she could no longer hear the sound of Mr. Clarke's ax. She looked at the great trees, the bushes, and the gently swaying bracken, but there was nothing that she could remember ever having seen before and she knew then with a sense of desolation that she was lost. She was unaware of how long she had been looking for kindling and she wondered if Mr. Clarke and Ben were searching for her, but no one was calling her name. She felt a moment of terror, and she thought of Mrs. Clarke sitting at home in the living room with her sewing, and of Davy asleep in the wicker cradle. She pushed her way through the bracken, not knowing which direction she should take, but hoping that each step would bring her nearer to Mr. Clarke and Ben. The bundle of firewood in her arms had grown heavy, but having found so much kindling she was determined not to leave any of it in the forest.

She splashed through some water, and then, as she looked down, she remembered the stream and the stick that she had sent floating away to join the river, in the hope that it would be carried down to the waterfall. She knew that the stream could lead her back to the clearing, and she began to follow the course of the water. Still clutching the bundle of kindling, she went steadily on, scrambling under low branches and avoiding nettles and trailing brambles.

Sometimes with a great flapping of wings, birds flew up from the undergrowth, indignant at being roused from their slumbers, frightening her so much that some of the pieces of kindling fell from her arms. She felt that she was being pursued by something strange and terrible, but everywhere there seemed to be bushes and trees barring her path. Suddenly she tripped and fell with her face pressed against the pile of kindling, but then, as she lay trying to recover her breath, she heard the sound of Mr. Clarke's ax, and, overjoyed, she hurried through the bushes to the clearing. Ben was there, too, tying the kindling into bundles.

"All right, then, Hester?" asked Mr. Clarke.

"Yes, Pa," said Hester thankfully. She thought that she had been lost for several hours.

"You've a good load of firewood there," said Mr. Clarke. "Let Ben make it up into bundles for you."

When Hester placed the kindling on the ground, she saw that it was larger than the pile that Ben had collected, and she felt a momentary triumph which made up for the feeling of dread she had experienced when she thought she was lost. She made up her mind that if ever she came to the forest again, she would be careful not to venture too far by herself.

"That's about it, then," Mr. Clarke said, after he had cut the number of stakes that he thought would be needed to repair his fencing. He separated them into two bundles and tied them securely with rope. He would have to make two journeys to the wheelbarrow at the edge of the forest, each time carrying a bundle of stakes on his shoulders. When he set off, Hester and Ben walked by his side, each with a pile of kindling, and when they came out from the forest, Mr. Clarke loaded everything into the wheelbarrow.

"You can stand guard while Ben and I go back for the rest of the things, Hester," he said.

"Yes, Pa," said Hester. As Ben and his father disappeared back into the forest, she stood by the wheelbarrow looking across the fields to the yard and the outbuildings of the Clarkes' house. Beyond them she could see the fields of Pollitt's Spread and the farmhouse, and then the clusters of houses, the schoolhouse, and the church which formed the village of Silver Falls. She thought of the men and women who had landed at Halifax and had gradually made their way inland, cutting down the trees and digging out great roots and huge stones from the red soil. In spite of cold, hunger and illness, houses had been built, homes created, and crops sown and harvested through the years. Hester thought of the courage of the early pioneers, which had sustained them through so many hardships.

When Ben and his father came back, Mr. Clarke swung the second bundle of stakes down from his shoulders onto the wheelbarrow with a sigh of contentment. He wiped his forehead with his hand, and Hester knew that the load must have been very heavy. He went back again into the forest for the ax, and Ben brought the last of the firewood, and then they all walked back through the fields.

"Is everyone safe and sound?" asked Mrs. Clarke when Hester came into the living room.

"Yes, Ma," said Hester, smiling. She was glad to be home again.

One morning in the yard before school began, Lottie told Hester that her sister Rachel would be coming home on Wednesday. "Remember that I told you she went to Millford to look after Aunt Min?" said Lottie. "Well, Aunt Min's been on the mend for some time now, and she's well enough to take on the housekeeping again, so it's all been fixed up for Rachel and Will to be married at the end of the month."

It was Ben's turn to do the afternoon milking that week, so after school there was no need for Hester to hurry back home. On Wednesday afternoon she and Lottie and Jim walked leisurely out from the school yard, and when they turned the corner and came into the main street, a buggy with a man and a young woman sitting in it had just stopped outside the Savins' store.

"It's our Rachel and Will," said Lottie delightedly. "Rachel!" she called out, and she and Jim ran across the road to the buggy where Will was helping Rachel to step down from the front seat. As Hester stood on the sidewalk she thought how smart Rachel looked in her gray bonnet and dark-blue mantle. Rachel kissed Lottie and Jim, and then the door of the store was suddenly opened and Mr. and Mrs. Savin came hurrying onto the sidewalk. Mrs. Savin held out her arms and Rachel ran and clung to her. Although Will had driven into Millford once a week to see Rachel and Mr. Savin had called in at his brother's house each month when he went to the town for more provisions for the store, Mrs. Savin had not seen her elder daughter since that day in April when Rachel had gone to live in Millford.

"You're looking well," Mrs. Savin said, smiling at the happy face framed in the gray bonnet.

"It's good to be back home, Ma," said Rachel.

Will lifted a trunk and a bonnet box down from the back of the buggy, and he and Mr. Savin carried them into the store, and then Mrs. Savin and her children went inside. Hester remembered her own arrival in Silver Falls, with her few possessions wrapped in a regulation black shawl. More than three months had passed since she and Bethanne had driven into the village with Mr. Clarke, both thinking of the home that had been offered to them, and of the people with whom they would live. She thought again of Mrs. Clarke's kind welcome on that afternoon, and she wondered if the Giffords had been able to make Bethanne feel that there was a special place for her within their household.

Once during the morning recess at school, Hester had asked Lottie about Mapletown.

"It's some way from here," Lottie had said. "I reckon it must be all of fifteen miles. Too far to go visiting, I should think."

Hester was disappointed to learn that Mapletown was so far away from Silver Falls. Although she was glad that Lottie was her friend, she would never forget Bethanne, and she hoped that one day they would be able to meet again.

The next day Lottie told her of some of the things that Rachel had brought home from Millford. The two sisters were sharing a bedroom, and she had been allowed to watch as Rachel unpacked the trunk. Uncle Jack and Aunt Min had no children, and they were both very grateful to her for all the work she had done during the months she lived with them. Aunt Min had given her a tea service, and from Uncle Jack there was a gift of money which had surprised Rachel by its amount, and which she and Will would use to help stock their small farm. While staying in Millford, Rachel had made her wedding dress. Only Mrs. Savin had been allowed to see it, and then it had been put away in the big chest in her bedroom.

"There's a whole pile of sewing to be done," said Lottie. "Ma said that Rachel was to have the patchwork quilt off the bed. It's only fair really, because she made it when she was still at school. She was always good with her needle—just like you, Hester. Ma said that it's about time I finished my own quilt." She sighed, and thought ruefully of her patchwork. "The trouble is," she said, "Ma's so particular. Sometimes I think I'll never get it finished, not even by the time I'm grown up and going to be married."

Hester's patchwork was progressing steadily, because

whenever she brought it down from the loft into the living room, she added at least six pieces to the quilt, and sometimes more if there were no other household tasks for her to do. Most of the small pieces of material that she had found in the ragbag were in plain, dark colors. She had used Mrs. Pollitt's bright-red cloth very sparingly, and sometimes when she looked at the squares of black, brown, gray, and dark green, she remembered Lady Talbot's purple mantle and she thought how the royal color would have brightened up the quilt.

After church on Sunday afternoon, Mrs. Savin and Rachel came to speak to Mrs. Clarke.

"Pleased to see you again, Rachel," said Mrs. Clarke. "I expect that you're going to be busy during the next week or two."

"Yes," said Rachel, smiling. "That's what Ma and I want to ask you about. We were wondering if your Hester could come and spend next Saturday with us and help with some of the sewing. Lottie's told us what a good needlewoman she is."

Mrs. Clarke looked pleased and glanced at Hester. "Would you like to go, Hester?" she said.

"Yes, please, Ma," said Hester.

"Will's mother is coming as well," said Mrs. Savin. "We'll have a whole day at it."

Hester was glad that Rachel and Mrs. Savin had asked her to go to their house, and she looked forward to the Saturday sewing bee.

"I'll see you tomorrow, then," Lottie said on Friday afternoon when school ended. "Ma said to come as early as you can after breakfast."

"All right, Lottie," said Hester. "I'll be there."

She arrived at the Savins' store at half past eight. Lottie

was there to meet her, and they went up the narrow, scrubbed staircase to the bedroom that Rachel was sharing with Lottie.

"Hello, Hester," said Rachel. "Let me take your things."

"Thank you, Rachel," Hester said.

"There's not going to be much room, I'm afraid," said Rachel cheerfully, as she hung Hester's bonnet and shawl on a nail on the back of the door. "We'll have to let Ma and Mrs. Cairns have the chairs. Would you like to sit on the bed?"

"Thank you," said Hester. In the bedroom there was a table with a china jug and basin standing on it, a big chest, and a bed covered with the patchwork quilt that Rachel had made when she was at school. By the bed there was a small rug made of looped cloth. Two straight-backed chairs had been brought up from the living room downstairs for Mrs. Savin and Mrs. Cairns.

"We measured the sheets last night," said Rachel. "Would you like to make a start on the hemming? Help yourself to a needle and thread from the workbasket on the shelf."

After Hester had threaded a needle, Rachel went to the chest where there was a pile of sheeting ready to be hemmed. She gave one sheet to Hester and then took one for herself, and then they sat together on the bed and began stitching the long hems. Lottie sat on the rug with the sewing with which she had been entrusted. She had already made a long bolster and was busy sewing a pillow.

"Good morning, Hester," said Mrs. Savin, when she came into the bedroom.

"Good morning, ma'am," said Hester, looking up from her work for a moment.

"I'm glad that you were able to come," said Mrs. Savin,

as she sat down in one of the chairs and began to work on another piece of sheeting. When Mrs. Cairns arrived, she was escorted up to the bedroom by Tom.

"Good morning, everybody," she said, and the other members of the sewing bee stopped working and greeted her. Will's mother was a small woman. She had brought with her a large basket which Tom placed on the floor. The contents of her basket were covered with a black cloth. Rachel helped her take off her brown bonnet and cloak, under which she was wearing a dark-gray dress and a green striped apron. Her gray hair was drawn back into a knot in the nape of her neck.

"I meant to be here a good bit earlier than this, Mrs. Savin," Mrs. Cairns said, "but have you ever known anyone so helpless about victuals as menfolk? Pa and the boys will make do with bread and cheese for midday, but I couldn't trust any of them with the supper for tonight, so I stayed and prepared everything just ready for them to put on the stove. Now you know what you're letting yourself in for with our Will, Rachel," she added, but both she and Rachel laughed, and no one seemed at all worried.

"I don't think that you know Hester," said Mrs. Savin.

"You mean the girl from up at the Clarkes'?" said Mrs. Cairns, as Hester stood up. "I've seen you in church, Hester. I'm pleased to meet you."

"Thank you, ma'am," Hester said. Mrs. Cairns looked appraisingly at her, but Hester thought that there was kindness and sympathy in her dark-brown eyes.

"How are you getting on with the bolster set, young Lottie?" said Mrs. Cairns, as Hester sat down.

"The bolster's ready, ma'am," said Lottie, "and I've just started on one of the pillows."

"Well, I've brought the filling," said Mrs. Cairns. When

she removed the black cloth from the basket, everyone could see that it was tightly packed with brown and white feathers. "I've been saving feathers for quite a time now, long before Rachel and Will were promised," said Mrs. Cairns. "There's plenty back home up in the loft if you need any more, Rachel."

"Thank you, Mrs. Cairns," Rachel said.

"Well, now," said Will's mother. "It seems as if I've had my say, and now I'd best get started on some sewing. You all seem to be putting me to shame." She took a thimble from the pocket of her apron and sat down on the chair next to Mrs. Savin. She admired the quality of the sheeting and then began working.

The three grown-ups and the two girls sewed until twelve o'clock, and then Mrs. Savin and Lottie went downstairs to prepare lunch. During the morning, as everyone was busy, Hester remembered the long, silent afternoons in the sewing room at the asylum with Miss Brown, and as she glanced around the bedroom, she thought that the sewing bee was a very happy occasion. Although she would have been very content to listen to what everyone else had to say, Rachel always ensured, with a smile and a few kind words, that she was included in the conversation, and Hester thought that it was almost as if she were a member of the Savin family. Will's mother and Mrs. Savin spoke of the preparations that they had made for their own weddings.

"It's a good many years ago now," said Mrs. Cairns, "but at home in the linen chest there's still one of the pillowcases I made in the winter before Gideon and I were wed." In a Bible on a small table in her living room there was a pressed flower from the posy she had carried on her wedding day.

"Rachel and Will are starting off with more than Nathaniel and I did," said Mrs. Savin, remembering the early days in England.

"I know that we've been lucky, and we're grateful," said Rachel, and she was thinking not only of the sheets and pillows, but also of the gifts from Uncle Jack and Aunt Min.

For lunch there were mashed potatoes, pickles, and boiled bacon. When Hester, Rachel, and Mrs. Cairns went downstairs to the living room, Jim was already sitting at the table, and then Tom and Mr. Savin came in from the store.

"They're not working you too hard, I hope, Hester?" asked Mr. Savin.

"No, sir," said Hester, realizing how much she had enjoyed the morning.

When the meal was over, she and the three grown-ups went back upstairs, while Lottie washed the dishes. In addition to the sheets, there were pillowcases to be made, and towels and curtains to be hemmed. Lottie had made two pillows, and when she came into the bedroom she filled both of them and the bolster with the feathers from the basket. Mrs. Cairns had brought such a large quantity that when the last seam had been sewn, everyone commented on the luxurious appearance of Lottie's work. Lottie was pleased when Rachel thanked her. She had enjoyed filling the bolster and the pillows far more than the sewing. Mrs. Savin worked until five o'clock and then she went downstairs to prepare the evening meal. When Jim knocked on the bedroom door and said that it was ready, everyone went down to a special supper to celebrate the end of the sewing bee. There were potatoes and a chicken pie that Rachel had made, and then slices of fruit cake and mugs of coffee.

"We've had a right good day," said Mrs. Cairns, "and if that pie is anything to go by, Rachel, then I'd say that our Will's always going to be able to sit down to a good meal when he comes home from his work."

"Thank you, Mrs. Cairns," said Rachel, aware that everyone sitting around the table was looking fondly at her.

At half past seven it was time for Hester to go home. While she was upstairs with Lottie, putting on her bonnet and shawl, Rachel came into the bedroom.

"Thank you for coming today, Hester," she said. "I'm very grateful to you for all the work you've done."

"You're welcome, Rachel," Hester said.

"I'd like you to have something as a keepsake of my sewing bee," Rachel said. She went to the chest and took out a length of narrow blue velvet ribbon, and then held it against Hester's hair. "There you are. It's almost the color of your eyes," she said.

"Thank you," Hester said, and her voice trembled because the velvet ribbon was so soft and pretty.

"You must come visiting when Will and I are settled," said Rachel.

"Thank you, Rachel," said Hester. "I'd like to."

"And when it's your turn to have a sewing bee, I hope that you'll ask me to come up to Mrs. Clarke's and spend the day," Rachel said.

"Yes, I will," said Hester, wondering if the day would ever come when she had a sewing bee of her own.

"We'll go and say good-bye to Ma now," Lottie said. She was smiling as if she knew a secret. Hester said good-bye to Rachel and then she and Lottie went downstairs to the living room.

"Just off, then, Hester?" said Mrs. Savin.

"Yes, ma'am," Hester said.

"Tell Mrs. Clarke that we're obliged to her for letting you come," Mrs. Savin said. "You've been a big help to us today."

"Thank you," Hester said.

After she had said good-bye to Mrs. Cairns, she went with Lottie and her mother into the store. Mrs. Savin went to the counter and took two big sticks of candy from the tall glass jar.

"I want you to have these for all your hard work, Hester," she said.

Hester hesitated because she had already had lunch and supper with the Savins, and Rachel had just given her the blue velvet ribbon.

"Rachel gave you the ribbon for a keepsake," said Mrs. Savin kindly, "and this is something which you don't have to keep—from Pa, Lottie, and me."

"Thank you, Mrs. Savin," Hester said, looking down at the striped candy.

When she went home, only Mrs. Clarke was in the living room, so Hester told her all about the sewing bee, Mrs. Cairns' basket of feathers, and the special supper. Mrs. Clarke smiled when she saw the blue velvet ribbon. Hester placed the two sticks of candy on the table and asked Mrs. Clarke to put them in the jar on the dresser.

"Thank you, Hester," she said. "It's a long time since we had any candy from the store."

Rachel and Will Cairns were married at the end of the month. Everyone in Silver Falls went to the church, just as they did on every Sunday afternoon, but on this occasion the front pews were left empty for the relatives of the bride and the bridegroom. Hester and Mrs. Clarke with Davy on her lap sat at the end of the pew nearest the aisle. Mr. and Mrs. Cairns came in, nodding and smiling to their friends as they went up to the front of the church, where Will and his brother were waiting. Uncle Jack and Aunt Min had driven over from Millford, and they arrived with Lottie and Jim. Lottie looked very solemn, as if she had just realized that after the ceremony was over, her sister Rachel would be Mrs. Cairns and would drive off in the buggy with Will to her new home. Tom accompanied Mrs. Savin, who was wearing a freshly trimmed bonnet and a new shawl. The congregation stood up to sing the first hymn, and then Rachel and her father walked slowly up the aisle.

Hester looked up from her hymnbook as they passed the Clarkes' pew. Rachel's dress was made of white cotton sprigged with pink rosebuds. Her pink bonnet was tied with white ribbons, and she carried three white roses that had come from Mrs. Cairns's garden. Will looked back and smiled at Rachel, and then they both stood before the minister and said the marriage vows. It was very still in the church as everyone listened intently. Hester glanced once at Mrs. Clarke and saw the gentle expression in her eyes.

After the ceremony had ended, Will and Rachel walked down the aisle, smiling at everyone who had come to wish them well. There was a special smile from Rachel for Hester and Mrs. Clarke. Behind the bride and groom came their families. Tom and Lottie grinned at the Clarkes' pew, and Jim said, "Hello, Hester," quite loudly, as if quite unabashed by the solemnity of the marriage service.

When the congregation came out from the church, Rachel and Will were standing by their buggy, and their two families stood around, smiling and talking. Someone had tied a white bow to one of the shafts of the buggy. Most of Rachel's possessions, including the patchwork quilt and everything that had been made at the sewing bee, were already at the farmhouse, but in the back of the buggy were a few last-minute bundles and a basket of provisions from the store.

When it was time to leave, Rachel kissed Mr. and Mrs. Cairns, her aunt and uncle, Lottie and her brothers, then her father, and, last of all, Mrs. Savin. Mrs. Savin stood close to the buggy as Will helped Rachel up into the front seat.

"Good-bye, everybody," said Will.

"Thank you for everything," said Rachel. "Good-bye, Mr. and Mrs. Cairns. Good-bye, Pa. Good-bye, Ma."

"Good-bye," everyone called out, as Will and Rachel drove away. Mr. Savin looked at his wife, and she gave a brave smile and waved until the buggy with the fluttering white bow had passed out of sight. Then all the members of the congregation began to make their way home. Even though it was a special day, it would soon be time for the afternoon milking.

# Chapter 9

MR. CLARKE had sown some of his land with wheat and through the months of summer the field changed from pale green to bronze, and then faded to the color of parchment as the grain ripened. One evening he picked a stalk and rubbed the ear of wheat between his hands. After he had blown away the papery sheaths that covered the wheat, he pressed a grain between his thumb and forefinger. It was dry, and he knew that the field was ready to be cut.

In the barn the scythe and the reaping hook were re-sharpened and Mr. Clarke and Ben went out to the field. When Davy was asleep in the cradle, Hester and Mrs. Clarke helped with the harvesting. They bound the newly cut grain into sheaves and then set seven or eight of them together to form a shock. At first, Hester found the work rather hard. Among the wheat there were thistles that pricked her fingers and the jagged edges of the stubble hurt her hands, but she worked as quickly as she could, tying the sheaves and dragging them into position. The evening was very warm and the work was tiring, but everyone worked steadily, stopping to rest for only a few minutes. Hester and Mrs. Clarke stayed in the wheatfield until half past eight, but Ben and his father worked until it grew dark, and at the end of the sixth evening all the grain had been cut and was standing in shocks.

"Five or six days, as long as the weather holds," Mr. Clarke said, "and then we can bring it home." Hester smiled as she looked up at the sky. The gold-capped clouds against the sunset promised that the next day would be fine. She wanted everything to go well for the Clarkes. At the end of the six days when all the shocks had dried, Blackie pulled the cart into the field and stood patiently among the stubble while Mr. Clarke and Ben pitchforked the sheaves up into the cart, where Hester and Mrs. Clarke stood waiting to arrange them in neat rows. When the cart was piled high with the sheaves, Blackie pulled it back again to the yard, and Mr. Clarke and Ben began to build a grain rick. When all the sheaves had been brought home and the rick had been completed, Hester and the Clarkes looked at it with the same sense of thanksgiving that they had felt at haymaking time.

When their own harvesting was done, Mr. Clarke and Ben went to help the Pollitts. Hester would have liked to have gone too, but Mrs. Clarke told her that she must glean their own wheatfield, searching for any grain stalks that had not been gathered into a sheaf, so for the next few afternoons, as soon as she had milked Maggie, Hester put on her sunbonnet and went out into the field. Sometimes her back ached and her hands were sore from the sharp, coarse stubble, but she carefully went on working and was quite proud of the small bundles of wheat that she was able to take back home.

When the Pollitts' sheaves had been taken to the yard, George said that Hester and Ben could go gleaning in the fields belonging to Pollitt's Spread. It was one of the biggest farms in Silver Falls. Every morning, either George or Luke drove into the village with churns of milk, and twice a week Mrs. Pollitt placed a large wicker basket in the back of the cart and told whichever of her sons who happened to be driving to be careful, as everyone knew that the state of the road into Silver Falls wasn't all it should be, and no one in his right sense would pay full price for a cracked egg. The money earned from the eggs had always been considered to be Mrs. Pollitt's personal property, and she had been saving it steadily for several years.

Besides the pasture lands and the fields of wheat, the Pollitts also owned a large apple orchard, and the fruit was sold in Silver Falls and in Millford. Mrs. Pollitt had often said, "Waste not, want not," and when Hester and Ben went to Pollitt's Spread to glean the first wheatfield, she was already there, wearing her big sunbonnet and checked apron, and moving slowly through the stubble, her sharp eyes searching for any ears of wheat that had fallen from the sheaves. She looked up and waved when she saw Hester and Ben, and they waved back.

Ben went to the far end of the field and began gleaning. Hester had hoped that he would be a little more friendly when he saw that she tried to work as hard as everyone else did at home, and that she was anxious to earn the place which his parents had given her, but as they set out for Pollitt's Spread, although they walked side by side, Ben had not made any attempts at conversation, and Hester thought again of the happy relationship that existed between Lottie, Tom, and Jim.

As she began gleaning, she remembered that the Bible reading in church on Sunday afternoon had been about harvesting. Mr. Anderson had read the story of Ruth. She, too, had gleaned a wheatfield far away from the country where she had been born. Hester thought of the milking, the butter making, her cooking lessons, the hay season, and the wheat harvest, and it seemed to her that since coming to Silver Falls she had learned to do many new things.

Walking slowly through the field she was able to gather a small sheaf of wheat to take home to Mrs. Clarke. She was not sure when it would be time for supper, and so she waited until Ben came through the stubble. She saw him quickly glance at her sheaf, and she felt glad that she had found as much wheat as he had. They went gleaning on several evenings. Later in the year all the wheat would be threshed in the barns and then taken by cart into Millford to be ground at the mill.

Toward the end of the month there were the dusky red cranberries to be picked, and Hester and Mrs. Clarke went out to the fields with baskets, while Ben stayed at home and looked after Davy. Hester enjoyed the cranberry pie that Mrs. Clarke made for Sunday dinner, and she thought that cranberry sauce made a meal of boiled potatoes and cold meat seem something rather special. One afternoon when she came home from school, Mrs. Clarke asked her to pick some cranberries for Mrs. Pollitt.

"I know that George and Luke are very partial to cranberry sauce," she said.

"Yes, Ma," Hester said. In the small field the berries

were plentiful, and she soon filled her small basket. After showing them to Mrs. Clarke, she took the berries to Pollitt's Spread.

"Step inside," said Mrs. Pollitt, when Hester knocked on the back door of the farmhouse.

"Mrs. Clarke sent some cranberries for you, Mrs. Pollitt," said Hester.

"I'm much obliged to her," said Mrs. Pollitt. "Did you pick them?"

"Yes, ma'am," said Hester, as she gave the basket to her.

"Go on into the living room, then," said Mrs. Pollitt. "I'll put the berries into a dish."

Hester went into the living room of the farmhouse. She looked up at the six cups and saucers on the top shelf of the dresser, remembering how Mrs. Pollitt had told her that they had been brought all the way from England many years ago.

"Sit yourself down," said Mrs. Pollitt, when she came in from the pantry. "Rest for a spell."

"Thank you, ma'am," Hester said. She sat on a stool close to the rocking chair, aware of Mrs. Pollitt's steady examination of her face.

"You seem to be filling out," said Mrs. Pollitt, "and there's a nice bit of color in your cheeks. Life here in Silver Falls seems to agree with you. It's very different here from what it was in England, I expect."

"Yes, ma'am," said Hester. In all the weeks that she had lived in Silver Falls, Mrs. Clarke and her husband had never once asked her about the orphan asylum at Marcroft. In the parlor of the minister's house at Halifax, Miss Hayward had given Mr. Clarke a letter in which the matron had stated all that was known about Hester Fielding, and that first evening, when Hester was asleep up in the loft,

Mr. Clarke had read the few lines of the letter and then given it to his wife to read. Afterward Mrs. Clarke had put it away in the drawer in which she kept all the special things, next to a piece of paper in which was wrapped one of Ben's baby curls.

"Mrs. Clarke told me that you are right handy with your needle," said Mrs. Pollitt. "How's that patchwork coming along?"

"Quite well, thank you," said Hester. "I do some most evenings, except Sundays."

"Which is no more than it should be," said Mrs. Pollitt. "Sunday should always be kept as a day apart from all the rest. I hope that when my menfolk fix on somebody, they'll both choose a wife who's good with her needle. Still, if they don't, it won't be for want of me telling them." She stood up from her chair. "Well, I must pay my debts, I suppose," she said. "Will you take two eggs in return for what you've brought?"

Hester wriggled uncomfortably on the stool, because she had not expected to receive anything in return for picking the cranberries.

"As I've said before," went on Mrs. Pollitt, "there's no taste to nothing. You stay where you are, and I'll go across to the henhouse and see if I can find a couple of eggs."

She picked up the basket and went out into the farmyard, and Hester was left alone in the living room. She looked at the scrubbed floorboards, at the medicine cupboard, and at the stove with the big chimney pipe set in the wall. On one of the beams of the ceiling there was a pipe rack, and she wondered if George and Luke smoked, or whether it had belonged to Mrs. Pollitt's husband. On the table there was a workbasket in which there were a shirt and some socks, and she smiled as she thought of what Mrs. Pollitt had said about telling her sons to choose a wife who was a good needlewoman. She remembered Rachel Savin's sewing bee. She was not sure if either George or Luke was going out with anyone, but she thought that the young women whom they chose would be expected to be as capable as Mrs. Pollitt and know how to do everything, just as she did.

"I was lucky," said Mrs. Pollitt, when she came back from the yard. "There's two big brown eggs for you. They haven't been laid for more than a few minutes."

"Thank you, Mrs. Pollitt," Hester said.

"Mind you tell Mrs. Clarke that I'm obliged to her for thinking of me," said Mrs. Pollitt, as she gave Hester the basket. "And be careful how you go with those eggs. They don't come as easily as cranberries."

"Yes, ma'am," said Hester.

"Off you go, then," said Mrs. Pollitt. "I've got my work to do."

Hester knew that Mrs. Clarke would be pleased to receive the two eggs, and she carried the basket carefully back home.

At school the next day there was considerable excitement when Miss Foster told her pupils that one of her cousins who lived in England had sent her a parcel of books. There were three storybooks and three volumes of poetry. Hester and Lottie particularly admired the bindings of the poetry books. One even had a bookmark of narrow black velvet ribbon.

"If you promise to be very careful," said Miss Foster, "you can each take one home and keep it for a few days. Would you like that?"

"Yes, please, Miss Foster," said Hester and Lottie excitedly, and the teacher smiled, thinking that when she wrote a letter of thanks to her cousin she would tell him of the interest and pleasure that his generous gift had caused in the small schoolhouse in Silver Falls. When Hester showed Mrs. Clarke the book of poetry which Miss Foster had allowed her to bring home, the book and its ribbon bookmark were greatly admired.

"Take care of it while it's in your possession, Hester," Mrs. Clarke said.

"Yes, I will, Ma," Hester replied. After she had played with Davy, she sat reading the poems, not even looking up when Ben came into the living room after he had finished the milking. He sat at the table and began to draw. At about five o'clock someone knocked on the front door. When Ben opened it, Mrs. Pollitt was standing on the threshold.

"Come in, Mrs. Pollitt," said Mrs. Clarke.

"I'm obliged," said Mrs. Pollitt.

Hester looked up from her book and smiled shyly at her, but there was a cold, angry expression on Mrs. Pollitt's face.

"Won't you sit down?" said Mrs. Clarke.

"Thank you," said Mrs. Pollitt, "but I think it's best that I stand. I've come about my silver thimble. It's gone."

"I'm sorry to hear that," said Mrs. Clarke.

"I've looked everywhere," said Mrs. Pollitt, "but it's not to be found. I was wondering if Hester knows anything about it."

"Why should she?" said Mrs. Clarke quietly.

"She was over at my place yesterday," said Mrs. Pollitt. "In the evening when I took out my sewing, the thimble wasn't in its case."

Hester put the book of poems down on the table. Her hands were shaking.

"Do you know anything about Mrs. Pollitt's thimble, Hester?" Mrs. Clarke asked.

Hester was aware of the concern showing so clearly in Mrs. Clarke's eyes. She did not look at Ben, but she knew that he was staring at her.

"No, ma'am," she said, and although she was trembling, her voice was quite firm.

"You've heard Hester's reply, Mrs. Pollitt," said Mrs. Clarke, after a little while.

"Talk's cheap enough," Mrs. Pollitt said grimly. She looked at Hester. "Well, young woman, you were in the living room all by yourself when I went out to the yard to get those eggs. Are you sure that you don't know anything about my thimble?"

"Yes, ma'am," said Hester. She stood up and gripped the seams of her gown. "I sat on the stool all the time that you were out in the yard. I didn't touch anything."

There was a heavy silence in the living room. No one moved.

"All right," said Mrs. Pollitt. Her lips set into a thin line as she turned to Mrs. Clarke. "I'd rather have lost a mint of money than that thimble," she said. "It means a lot to me."

"I hope that it will soon be found, Mrs. Pollitt," said Mrs. Clarke.

"So do I," said Mrs. Pollitt, "and I trust that you and your husband won't ever have cause to regret that you took in a strange girl whom nobody knows anything about."

"I think that you've said enough," replied Mrs. Clarke.

"Have I?" said Mrs. Pollitt. "If that thimble is found here, I'd be obliged if you'd return it to me, and then that will be the end of the matter."

She glanced again at Hester, and then went out from the room.

Mrs. Clarke and Ben looked at Hester, who stood nervously twisting her hands.

"Would you go out to the barn and get some more wood, Ben, please?" asked Mrs. Clarke.

"Yes, Ma," said Ben, although he knew that the wood basket was still half full.

Hester stood by the table, looking at Mrs. Clarke.

"Sit down, Hester," Mrs. Clarke said, as Ben went out through the back door. Hester sat down again and waited for Mrs. Clarke to speak.

"It's only natural that Mrs. Pollitt should be upset because she's lost her thimble," said Mrs. Clarke. "Try to forget what she said, Hester."

"Yes, ma'am," said Hester. She sat with her hands clenched tightly in her lap, remembering Mrs. Pollitt's red, angry face.

"I suppose that everybody likes pretty things," said Mrs. Clarke. "I know that I do, and right this very minute I wish that I could have a silk dress in a really bright color, and a parasol, and some china that wasn't cracked or chipped—and lots more things as well. But however much I'd like to have them, I would never take anything that belonged to someone else. Part of the pleasure in having nice things is being able to get them out and show them to friends when they come visiting. If I'd taken anything that didn't belong to me, I'd always have to keep it hidden away, and I'd never be able to show it to anyone, in case they recognized it as really belonging to somebody else. There wouldn't be much pleasure in that. And what is really the most important thing of all, I'd have thrown away my good name—which is more dear to me than a whole row of silk dresses and a dozen tea services. I can save up my money for a new cup and saucer, or buy some material for a dress, but I can't ever buy a good name. That's something which is earned by being trustworthy and honest." She was silent for a moment and then she said, "Now, there's one question that I must ask you, Hester, and I want you to answer me truthfully. Do you know anything at all about Mrs. Pollitt losing her thimble?"

Hester's face was very white, and her lips were trembling.

"No, ma'am," she said.

"All right," said Mrs. Clarke. "I believe you. Now, go on with your reading, there's a good girl."

Hester picked up the book from the table, but she stared at the pages without being aware of the lines of the poetry, knowing that Mrs. Pollitt believed that she had taken the thimble. Ben had been in the living room, and he had heard everything that had been said. Hester wondered if he would tell Tom at school the next day, and if he would tell Lottie. Perhaps even Miss Foster would hear about it, too. She put the book on the dresser and sat on the floor by the cradle. Davy reached out for her hand and smiled at her as if nothing unpleasant had happened, but when Ben came back into the living room with an armful of wood, she wondered what he was thinking.

Mrs. Clarke began to prepare supper and Hester set the table in readiness for the meal. Once she glanced at Mrs. Clarke as she stood by the stove, and she saw the worried expression on her face. It seemed to Hester that it was just like her first afternoon in Silver Falls, when everything had been so strange and when Ben had laughed at her hair, but then there had been the kindness of Mrs. Clarke to help dispel her feeling of nervousness and the sense of desolation that had swept over her when Bethanne had driven away with Mr. Gifford.

She wondered if Mrs. Clarke had really believed her when she had said that she had not taken the thimble. Always she had looked forward to suppertime, when Mr. Clarke was there and they all sat around the table and he told them of what had happened at the lumberyard and asked the two children about what they had learned at school. When he came home, he greeted everyone as he always did, and she murmured, "Hello, Pa," but her voice was little more than a whisper. She was not very hungry, but she managed to eat the stew, hoping that Mrs. Clarke would not ask her to have a second helping. Mr. Clarke was aware that something was wrong and he glanced questioningly at his wife, but she gave a tiny warning nod and continued to speak of ordinary, everyday things.

When Davy was ready for bed, Hester took him into the big bedroom and tucked the blankets around him. Her throat ached and her eyes felt hot and heavy with unshed tears, but she sang the lullaby until Davy was asleep. When she went back into the living room, Mr. Clarke looked at her, and she knew that Mrs. Clarke must have told him about Mrs. Pollitt's visit.

"Ma's just been telling me about the trouble we had earlier on, Hester," he said.

"Yes, sir," said Hester.

"Ma also told me that you don't know anything about the missing thimble," said Mr. Clarke.

"No, I don't, sir," said Hester. Again there was silence in the room, and she knew that Mrs. Clarke and Ben were watching her.

"You're quite sure, now?" asked Mr. Clarke.

"Yes, sir," Hester said, as firmly as she could.

"All right, then, Hester," said Mr. Clarke. "In that case there's nothing more to be said." He turned to Ben. "Will you give me a hand in the barn, Ben, please?"

"Yes, Pa," Ben said, and he and his father went out. Mrs. Clarke took her workbasket from the dresser and Hester began to go on with her patchwork, but the bright-red material which had been the gift of Mrs. Pollitt only reminded her of the angry words that had been spoken. She made very little progress with her sewing that evening, because her head was aching and sometimes her hands shook. She was glad when Mrs. Clarke said that it was time for bed and she was able to fold her work and go up the ladder to the loft. She undressed quickly and put on her nightgown. After she had said her prayers, she lay in bed wondering if Mrs. Clarke would come up to tuck her in, as she always did, and it seemed a long time before she heard the sound of her footsteps on the ladder.

"Good night, Hester," she said. "Sleep tight."

"Good night, Ma," Hester whispered. She lay still, looking up at the rafters of the loft while Mrs. Clarke went down the ladder to the living room, and after Ben had gone to bed, she could hear the voices of his parents in the room below. She thought that they would be talking about the missing thimble. "Be careful never to give your benefactors any cause to regret their charity," the matron had said on the last morning at the asylum. Hester remembered what Mrs. Pollitt had said, and she was afraid that Mr. and Mrs. Clarke might decide to send her back to England, to the orphanage at Marcroft.

She wondered who would pay her passage, and remembering the kindness of Mr. Weston and his wife, she thought that perhaps she would have to stay at their house until she could be sent back to face the contempt of Lady Talbot and the disappointment of Mrs. Ruth Norton. Even if the asylum would take her back, when the time came for her to be found a position as a maidservant, the board of guardians would have difficulty in placing her, because no one would accept into their house someone who was considered to be a thief. Perhaps she would be like old Nan, and stay behind the gray walls of the orphanage forever, growing old and knowing that there was no other place for her in the outside world. Then she realized that instead of being able to return to the asylum, she would be sent to a reformatory.

"The reformatory is the place for all bad girls," Miss Brown had often said, when she complained of sewing that had been badly done. "I shouldn't be surprised if some of you don't end up there one day. Then you'll be sorry."

Hester lay awake for a long time, moving restlessly in her bed as she thought of the terrors of the reformatory. At last she went to sleep, but it did not seem very long before Mrs. Clarke called out that it was time to get up, and when Hester was fully awake, all the worry and fear of the day before seemed to be there in the loft waiting for her. Wearily she dressed and went down the ladder into the living room.

"Good morning, Ma," she said quietly.

"Good morning, Hester," replied Mrs. Clarke. She was preparing breakfast, just as she did every morning. The two lunch bundles were ready on the table and one of the kettles was steaming on the stove, but although everything appeared to be going on in the same way, Hester knew that the morning was different from all the others. The loss of the silver thimble seemed to cast a shadow over the room. She went into the bedroom and washed her face and hands and when she came back into the living room, Mrs. Clarke placed a bowl of porridge on the table.

"Thank you, Ma," Hester murmured as she sat down.

"Did you sleep all right?" asked Mrs. Clarke.

"Yes, thank you, Ma," Hester said, trying to forget how long she had lain awake, worrying and thinking of the reformatory. She felt her face redden as Mrs. Clarke looked at her before she turned back again to the stove.

Soon afterward Ben came hurrying in for his breakfast. "Good morning, Ma. Good morning, Hester," he said, but Hester knew that he had spoken only because his mother was in the living room.

"Off you go, then," said Mrs. Clarke when it was time to go to school, and Hester and Ben went down the cart track together. When they were out in the road, Ben ran on ahead, as he did every morning, and as Hester walked alone past the entrance to Pollitt's Spread, she wondered if Mrs. Pollitt would be looking out of the window, watching her as she went by. When she went into the school yard, Ben was talking to Tom, and Lottie was with him, holding Jim by the hand. Hester thought for a moment that Ben was telling them about the thimble, but when Lottie saw her, she came running over to the gate to say that a special oil lamp had arrived at her father's store the previous evening.

"It's so pretty," said Lottie. "Both Ma and me want Pa to put it in the parlor, but he says that it's to be shown in the store first, and then, if nobody buys it at the end of six weeks, we can have it for ourselves. Ma said that you can come in to see it on your way home from school this afternoon."

"Thank you, Lottie," said Hester. "I'd like to see it." She was glad that Ben had not said anything about the thimble.

She found it hard to work at her lessons that day. She kept thinking about the thimble, and wondering if she would be sent back to England. Several of the additions which she did were wrong, and three times Miss Foster had to tell her to pay attention, saying that if she had occasion to speak to her again, she would have to come out and stand in front of the whole class as a punishment. She looked at Hester's white, set face and told her to remain in the schoolhouse after lessons had ended, and at three o'clock, when the other children ran to the row of pegs searching for caps, bonnets, and shawls, Hester sat looking down at her desk. Lottie thought how ill her friend looked. It was almost as if she were going to get the fever.

"Off you go, everyone," said Miss Foster, and when all the children had gone, the teacher closed the schoolhouse door. Hester sat waiting for Miss Foster to call her to her desk, but instead the teacher came to where she was sitting.

"Is there something troubling you, Hester?" she said.

"No, Miss Foster," said Hester.

The teacher put her hand on Hester's forehead and was surprised to find how hot it was.

"Do you feel all right?" she asked.

"Yes, ma'am," Hester said.

"Well, until now I've had no complaint to make about your work or about your behavior in class," said Miss Foster, "but today it's almost as if another girl had been sitting in the desk with Lottie. Is there anything that you want to tell me?"

"No, ma'am," said Hester, in a harsh, dry voice. She could never tell anyone about the missing thimble.

"You get on all right with Ben, don't you?" said the teacher, remembering Hester's first day at school, when Ben had left her standing just inside the door.

"Yes, Miss Foster," said Hester quickly, not wanting Ben to get into any trouble because of anything she said. If he did, he might tell about Mrs. Pollitt's visit.

"I see," said Miss Foster, thinking that over the months, through the care and kindness of the Clarkes, the thin, pale child with the cropped hair had become a sturdy, bright-eyed girl. Hester would always possess a quiet manner, but she had shown herself to be quick and ready to learn, and gradually she had acquired a certain confidence. A reliable girl, Miss Foster had often thought.

"Well," she said, "I won't keep you any longer. But if there is anything that is worrying you, then tell Mrs. Clarke. She has a right to know, and whatever it is, I'm sure that it can be put right."

"Yes, Miss Foster," said Hester.

"You can go now," said the teacher. "And remember that tomorrow is another day, and that you can start all over again."

Hester went to the row of pegs for her bonnet and shawl.

"Thank you, ma'am," she said, and then she opened the door of the schoolhouse.

Miss Foster was not really satisfied with the answers that she had received to her questions. Although through her years of teaching she knew that boys were rarely demonstrative, she remembered that Ben had never seemed very friendly toward Hester. As she cleaned the blackboard, she wondered what he had really thought when his parents had told him that they were going to adopt an orphan girl from England. Yet Hester had said that everything was all right between them. The teacher felt that she could not intervene in what might be a private matter, but she wanted to help her pupil in any way she could. She would see what happened tomorrow.

When Hester went out into the yard, Lottie and Jim were waiting for her by the gate.

"I thought you'd never come," Lottie said. "I want to show you that lamp."

Hester managed to smile and she took hold of Jim's hand and they all hurried out to the sidewalk. Hester was grateful to Lottie for her cheerfulness. For one terrible moment in the schoolhouse, she had thought that she was going to cry in front of Miss Foster.

No customer coming into Mr. Savin's store could miss seeing the lamp. It was placed next to the glass jar that contained the sticks of candy.

"There it is," said Lottie. "Isn't it a beauty?"

"Oh, yes," said Hester. The lamp was made of brass, and the globe was a delicate pink. She thought how wonderful it would look standing on the table in the Clarkes' house.

Lottie's father was weighing tea.

"Mind you tell Pa Clarke about the lamp, Hester," he said. "Maybe he'll buy it for you."

Hester knew that she could never ask Mr. Clarke for anything at all, but she smiled in agreement.

"Oh, Pa," said Lottie. "You know we don't want anybody to buy the lamp. We want to keep it for ourselves."

"You'll never make a good storekeeper, Lottie," said Mr. Savin. "All the shelves out here would be empty, and the parlor would be crammed full to the ceiling with the things that you'd taken a fancy to."

"Oh, Pa," said Lottie again. "Come on through and see Ma," she said to Hester.

"Well, not this afternoon," said Hester. "I ought to be getting home. I'm late enough already."

"All right," said Lottie. "I'll see you tomorrow, then." She went to the door with Hester. "And don't go fretting about school and Miss Foster," she said.

"No," said Hester, thinking that she would never worry about school and Miss Foster, because she enjoyed the work and she liked the teacher. While she had been in Mr. Savin's store looking at the lamp, for a few minutes she was able to forget her worries, but when she passed Pollitt's Spread on her way home, all her fears of the previous evening returned.

"Have you had a good day, Hester?" said Mrs. Clarke, when Hester came into the living room.

"Yes, thank you, Ma," Hester said quietly. She went over to the row of pegs and began to untie her bonnet strings.

"You're still worrying about Mrs. Pollitt, aren't you?" said Mrs. Clarke.

"Yes, ma'am," said Hester forlornly.

"Yesterday I asked you to try to forget what Mrs. Pollitt said. Remember that she's grieved about her loss, and things were said which shouldn't have been. I don't want you worrying so that everything's spoiled for you," said Mrs. Clarke.

"I thought that you might want to send me back," said Hester.

"Did you, Hester?" said Mrs. Clarke gently. "Do you remember the day when you first came to Silver Falls?"

"Yes, Ma," Hester said. She thought that she would always remember that day, for as long as she lived.

"I told you then that Mr. Clarke and I wanted you to call us Pa and Ma, and that you were to think of this house as your home," went on Mrs. Clarke. "We want you to be our own girl, and this is where you belong. So don't think anymore about being sent back to England."

"No, Ma," said Hester.

"Do you think that you can get all your additions right tomorrow?" asked Mrs. Clarke.

Hester knew that Ben must have told his mother of what had happened at school.

"Yes, Ma," she said. She could do anything for Mrs. Clarke.

"You haven't forgotten how to smile, have you?" said Mrs. Clarke.

"No, Ma," said Hester, but she was afraid that she might cry instead. "I wish Mrs. Pollitt would find her thimble," she said.

"So do I," said Mrs. Clarke. "We all do. Now, go and play with Davy. I expect that he's been wondering where you'd got to."

"Thank you, Ma," Hester said, and there was no longer a shadow in the living room.

At school the next day all her additions were correct.

"Well done, Hester," said Miss Foster.

# Chapter 10

*A*LTHOUGH HESTER KNEW that Mr. and Mrs. Clarke were quite certain that she had not taken Mrs. Pollitt's thimble, she was not sure that Ben believed that she knew nothing about its disappearance. Sometimes she was aware of him looking at her, and there was a strange watchful expression in his eyes that made her feel uncomfortable, and her face reddened as if she really were guilty.

Sunday afternoon, as they all drove to church in the buggy, she wondered if Mrs. Pollitt would be at the service. When she and Mrs. Clarke and Davy went inside, Mrs. Pollitt, George, and Luke were already there, sitting in their pew near the front of the church. Hester was glad when the blacksmith and his wife came and sat in the seat in front of the Clarkes' pew and she could no longer see Mrs. Pollitt's bonnet, but the pleasure that she had always found in the words and music was dimmed because of the missing thimble. After the service the members of the congregation stood outside the church for a few moments, speaking to their neighbors and friends. Mrs. Pollitt nodded to Mrs. Clarke and said, "Good afternoon."

"Good afternoon, Mrs. Pollitt," Mrs. Clarke said, and Hester stood close to her, thinking that it was the hardest thing in the world to pretend that there was nothing wrong between the Clarkes and the mistress of Pollitt's Spread. Mrs. Pollitt pursed her lips and then went over to the buggy and sat waiting for George and Luke, who were talking in their slow, easy manner to Mr. Clarke and Ben, just as if it had been an ordinary Sunday afternoon. As Hester went with Mrs. Clarke to their own buggy, she wondered if Mrs. Pollitt had told her sons about the missing thimble, and if they, too, believed that she had taken it.

The next day when she was walking home from school, Luke came by in the buggy after driving down to Mr. Savin's store, and he stopped and told her to climb up into the seat beside him. Hester hesitated at first, because she thought that Mrs. Pollitt would probably be looking out of the window and see her in the buggy when Luke reached the track that led to Pollitt's Spread, but Luke said, "Up you get, then, and we'll be back home in no time at all."

"Thank you," said Hester, as she sat down beside him.

"I thought that I might see Ben as well," said Luke, and she explained that it was her week to do the afternoon milking and that Ben had probably gone off with Tom Savin.

Luke was wearing an old straw hat with a broken brim.

"If you've some work to do when you get home," he said, "I'll take you all the way."

In spite of Luke's friendly conversation, Hester kept

thinking about the thimble, and she felt very uncomfortable when the buggy passed the entrance to Pollitt's Spread.

"Thank you very much, Mr. Pollitt," she said, when they reached the Clarkes' gate. "It was very good of you to bring me all the way home."

"Glad to have met you on the road," replied Luke, gallantly tipping his hat, and then he drove off to the farmhouse.

"You're back early, Hester," said Mrs. Clarke, when Hester went into the living room for her milking cap and apron.

"Mr. Luke Pollitt gave me a ride home," Hester said.

"Did he, now?" Mrs. Clarke said. "That was right neighborly of him."

Mrs. Pollitt had not told her two sons about the missing thimble. She had not told anyone. When she had driven away from the Clarkes' house, she thought of the words that she had spoken in anger because of her grief at her loss. She felt uneasy as she remembered the expression on Hester's face as she stood nervously fingering the seams of her gown. Then she thought of the thimble and how it had been prized so much by her mother, and it was for that reason, and not because it was made of silver, that it was especially dear to her. Whatever that girl may say, she thought, all I know is that the thimble's missing, and she was alone in the living room of my house, while I went out to the yard to fetch a couple of eggs. At supper that night she said very little and was not very hungry.

"Is anything wrong, Ma?" asked Luke, as he handed her his plate for another helping of potatoes.

"No, I'm all right," Mrs. Pollitt said, although she had eaten very little of her supper.

"We've told you before," said George. "There's no need for you to be doing too much."

When Mrs. Pollitt saw the look of anxiety on the faces of her two sons, for a moment she wanted to tell them of what had happened and what had been said in the Clarkes' house. Then she looked across the room to where the empty thimble case lay on top of her workbasket, and she thought again of her mother. There had been many times during the early days in Silver Falls when Mrs. Pollitt had felt lonely, and it seemed to be an almost impossible task to clear the land and start a small farm. She had been homesick, but she was always careful to encourage her husband when times were hard, and he never realized that her determination and cheerfulness had so often masked a desperate longing to return to England. The thimble and the six cups and saucers had been a comfort to her all through the years because they were reminders of home. Mrs. Pollitt sighed and looked up at her two sons.

"I'm all right," she said again. "I guess I'm just a bit tired, that's all."

Early in October Mr. Clarke and Ben picked all the apples from the two trees in the front garden, and Hester and Mrs. Clarke inspected them carefully to see that none was bruised or blemished in any way. All the sound apples were carefully wiped with a piece of cloth and then were laid on two wooden racks and stored in the loft. When Hester awoke each morning, there was the heavy, sweet scent of the mellow fruit coming from the corner of the room. Every year the crop was stored in the loft, but to Hester it seemed that the rows of apples were an assurance from Mr. and Mrs. Clarke that they trusted her and believed that she knew nothing of Mrs. Pollitt's missing thimble.

The weeks went by without Mrs. Clarke's receiving a visit from Mrs. Pollitt. Hester did not know if Mrs. Clarke had ever told her husband this, but she herself knew, because in the past when she had come home on Wednesday afternoon, there was usually a paper bag of candy on the dresser, which had been left by Mrs. Pollitt at the end of her visit. Each Wednesday afternoon she looked on the dresser, thinking that if she could see some candy there, it would mean that Mrs. Pollitt had at last called again, and that the thimble had been found, but October and November passed without a visit from Mrs. Pollitt. Sometimes when Hester sat playing with Davy, she wondered if Mrs. Clarke would ask Mrs. Pollitt to come if ever he had the colic or fever, or if she would send into Millford for Dr. Hall. When Mrs. Pollitt met Mrs. Clarke at church on Sunday afternoon she said, "Good afternoon," and that was all.

"A mild winter so far," people said, but one morning in the beginning of December, when Hester opened the shutters of the window in the loft, she could see that the first snow had fallen. Everything was white, except for the forest, which seemed blue-black against the gray sky. Sleighs were brought out from the back of the barns and the livestock was sheltered in the cow sheds and stables. Icicles hung from the eaves of the houses, and when Mr. Clarke, Ben, and Hester set out for the village each day, they wore snowshoes to prevent their feet from sinking into the snow.

At school the children were to give a concert for their parents on the evening of the day that school ended for the Christmas holidays. For several afternoons they had been rehearsing all the items that would make up the entertainment. Everyone was going to take part, even the three four-year-olds who always sat in the front of the class. They were to sing an action song about fish swimming in the river.

On the day of the concert the children spent the afternoon decorating the schoolhouse for the performance in the evening. The desks were pushed back to the end of the room, and two benches were brought from the church and placed just below the platform, where all the performers would sit waiting until it was time to say their poem or sing their song. The girls hung up decorations of spruce and fir cones, and on the blackboard Ben drew a picture of Joseph and Mary in the stable at Bethlehem. Mary knelt by the crib, and in the doorway of the stable were three shepherds. Miss Foster had brought one of the potted plants from her parlor and placed it on her desk.

When everything was ready, the children hurried home for the afternoon milking. In most homes that evening supper was served earlier than it usually was, and then the boys and girls returned to the schoolhouse. Ben and Hester walked through the snow together. Ben was carrying a lantern and trudged companionably by Hester's side. Although he said nothing, Hester was glad that he had not left her to make her way down to the village in the dark.

In the schoolhouse there was a great feeling of excitement as the time drew near for the parents to arrive. Mr. and Mrs. McCann came first, and then Miss Foster told her pupils to sit down on the benches and to be quiet. Even then there was a lot of whispering and nudging as other parents came. The mothers squeezed themselves into the desks, and the fathers stood leaning against the walls of the schoolroom.

Hester and Lottie sat together. Lottie kept looking to see if her parents had arrived, and when they did she waved to them. Hester could hear the people coming in, but she thought that it would be better if she did not turn around and stare. Lottie looked back each time that the door of the schoolhouse opened. "There's your ma and pa coming in just now," she said.

Hester turned and waved, and then settled in her seat with a pleased, excited feeling. She was the last performer in the concert and would read the Christmas story just before the minister said the prayers. She knew what she had to do and say. The big, black Bible was ready on Miss Foster's stand, with a green ribbon marking the place in St. Luke's gospel. In spite of the cold, Hester had practiced up in the loft, whispering so that no one would hear her, in order that it would be a surprise for Mr. and Mrs. Clarke on the night of the concert. She did not know where or when Ben had rehearsed, but at the practice that morning, he had been word-perfect. She glanced over to where he was sitting with Tom Savin. He seemed quite calm, although his hands were twisted in his lap.

Mr. Anderson took out his pocket watch and then he looked across the room to Miss Foster, who was sitting at the edge of the platform with all the songs and poems written out on pieces of paper, so that she could prompt anyone who might forget his or her words. The teacher smiled and nodded to Bill Masters, who stepped up onto the platform, ready to say the poem of welcome that had been written by Miss Foster. After he had cleared his throat, the audience was suddenly quiet. When Bill came to the end of the poem, everyone clapped and he stepped down from the platform grinning with relief and pleasure.

Then it was the turn of the three four-year-olds. They sang their song in shrill, piping voices and acted everything out, just as Miss Foster had taught them. At the end

*181*

of the song they were supposed to pretend to swim off the platform. Instead of turning to the left, Ned Huett turned to the right and ended up in Miss Foster's lap, but everyone laughed and the teacher didn't seem to mind.

Mary Richards was next, and she performed a folk dance while old Mr. Thatcher from The Apple Tree played the fiddle. Then it was Ben and Tom's turn, and they acted a sketch in which Ben played the part of an old farmer, and Tom was a man from the city who was trying to poke fun at the farmer just because he lived in the country. The audience laughed when the farmer was able to show that he was a lot smarter than the man from the city. At the end, when Ben and Tom jumped down from the platform, Lottie nudged Hester and they clapped with everyone else.

The room was quite still when Nell Cameron sang an old Scottish lullaby. The settlers who had come from Scotland thought of their relatives and friends and of the farms and villages where they had once lived. Jeff Butcher said the first verse of his poem and then was unable to remember the beginning of the second. He looked at Miss Foster.

" 'But where the surging waters fall,' " said Miss Foster.

"No, it ain't, Miss Foster," Jeff said. "That's the third verse."

The children gasped and moved excitedly on the benches. No one dared to argue with Miss Foster. They looked at the teacher and wondered what she would say.

"You're quite right, Jeff," said Miss Foster. "I've skipped a verse. I'm sorry."

"That's all right, Miss Foster," said Jeff consolingly. "Anyway, I've remembered how the second verse starts now. Shall I go on?"

"Yes, please," said Miss Foster, and Jeff went on to say the rest of the poem without a single mistake.

The program of songs and poems continued until nearly all the children had performed. Then there were only two pupils left, Lottie and Hester. Lottie walked to the platform and said the title of her poem. That was all that she was able to say. Instead of speaking the opening lines of the first verse, she just stood there and shook with laughter. She said the title of the poem again, but still went on laughing.

"Come on, Lottie," Mrs. Savin called out from the back of the room. "Get on with it. You've said it to me at home enough."

"I can't, Ma," Lottie gasped. "I feel just as if I was going to burst."

Mrs. Savin's reply was smothered by the great roar of laughter from everyone in the schoolhouse. "Well, all right, then," Mrs. Savin said, when she could at last make herself heard. "If you can't say it, then I will." She stood up and said the poem all the way through without any hesitation, and Lottie watched her with an expression of pride and wonder on her face. Everyone applauded when Mrs. Savin sat down and Lottie clapped loudest of all.

The room was quiet again when Hester went to Miss Foster's bookstand and opened the Bible. She looked out to where Mrs. Clarke was sitting, and in the audience she saw Mrs. Pollitt, who had also come to the Christmas concert in the schoolhouse. Their eyes met, and then Mrs. Pollitt looked down at her hands. Hester remembered what Mrs. Pollitt had said on the day that she had come to the Clarkes' house, and she thought that she was probably thinking that someone like her was the very last person who should be reading from the Bible. There was an expectant silence in the room as everyone waited for Hester to begin the reading, but her hands were shaking and she felt unable to speak. She glanced down at the open Bible, and the letters of the words seemed to be twisting themselves into unrecognizable shapes. Then she looked again at Mrs. Clarke, who sat at the back of the room, willing her to do well. Hester took a deep breath to steady herself.

"The reading is taken from the New Testament, from the Gospel according to St. Luke, Chapter Two, verses one to twenty," she said. She began quietly, and then her voice rose clearly and confidently in the crowded room. There was silence when she came to the end of the reading and closed the Bible. She did not expect to receive any applause, because clapping for someone who had read from the Bible might be considered to be lacking in respect for the Word of God. But she had her reward, all the same. Before she stepped down from the platform she looked again at Mrs. Clarke and saw the expression on her face.

"Thank you, Hester," said Mr. Anderson. Then he said two prayers and the concert came to an end. Everyone sat down again and the minister thanked Miss Foster and the children for their hard work, which had made the entertainment such a success. Suddenly there was a loud knocking on the door of the schoolhouse.

"Whoever can that be, Miss Foster?" said Mr. Anderson.

"I don't know, sir," replied Miss Foster, smiling.

"Would you send someone to see who's there?" said Mr. Anderson.

"Yes," said Miss Foster. "Bill Masters, would you go and see who it is, please?"

Everyone watched as Bill went to open the door. There

was nobody outside, but on the threshold there was a big basket covered with a white cloth.

"Ain't nobody here, Miss Foster," said Bill, grinning. "Only this big basket."

"Do you think that it's meant for us, Bill?" asked the teacher.

"There's a piece of paper on the basket, Miss Foster," said Bill. "It says 'For the children of Silver Falls.'"

"You'd better bring it in, then, Bill," said Miss Foster. She spoke very seriously, but she looked at the minister and laughter twinkled in her eyes. Bill picked up the basket and placed it on the teacher's desk. She lifted off the white cloth and inside the basket there were a pile of red apples and small packages of candy. Mrs. Anderson helped Miss Foster to distribute the gifts from the basket. There were an apple and a package of candy for all the children, even for those who were not yet old enough to attend school. Hester wondered where the basket had come from, and she thought that Miss Foster and the Andersons knew more about the Christmas gifts than they were willing to admit.

When it was time to go home, the boys went to the row of pegs for their caps, mufflers, and coats, and the girls began to put on their bonnets and cloaks. When Hester looked across the room, Mrs. Pollitt was just leaving the schoolhouse, and she felt a sense of relief as the black-clad figure disappeared into the darkness. Mrs. Clarke was talking to Mrs. Savin.

"Your Hester did very well for herself, and young Ben, too," said Mrs. Savin. "Which is more than can be said for our Lottie."

"But you did very well, Mrs. Savin," said Mrs. Clarke.

"Did I?" said Mrs. Savin. She laughed, thinking of how she had stood up in the audience and said the long poem all the way through without making any mistakes. "Now I come to think of it, I suppose I did."

"Hello, Ma," said Lottie, as she and Hester came to join Mrs. Clarke and Mrs. Savin.

"Aren't you ashamed of yourself, Lottie?" said Mrs. Savin, but the sparkle in her eyes belied the severity of her words.

Lottie grinned. "Yes," she said, "but I was proud of you, Ma. You said the poem far better than I ever would."

"That's what comes from all that rehearsing," said Mrs. Savin. "Did you know what your two were going to do, Mrs. Clarke?"

"No," said Mrs. Clarke, looking at Hester. "It was a complete surprise, but it was worth waiting for." Hester smiled and thought of all the whispered readings in the loft.

Tom and Ben were talking to Mr. Anderson, but when he saw that Mrs. Savin was looking for her son, he sent the boys over to where Mrs. Savin and Mrs. Clarke were waiting.

"You both did very well," said Mrs. Clarke.

"Hester's reckoned to be the best reader in the whole school," said Tom.

On the way home, Ben sat with his father in the front of the sleigh, and Hester and Mrs. Clarke and Davy, wrapped in sacks and old blankets, sat in the back. As they drove past Pollitt's Spread, a lamp glowed warmly in the darkness, and Hester thought again of the thimble that had somehow disappeared.

On Christmas Eve there was a strange excitement in the living room. Hester remembered Christmas at the orphan asylum and thought of the special lunch and dinner which the girls were told had been provided by the generosity of the taxpayers of Marcroft. There had been roast beef and plum pudding, and oranges and sweets. As the girls grew older, they made the small bag of sweets last as long as possible by eating only one sweet each day.

When Hester put Davy to bed, she sang two of the carols that she had learned at school, and in the living room Mr. Clarke and his wife glanced at each other, thinking how sweet Hester's voice sounded. When it was bedtime, Mrs. Clarke said, "I'll call you when breakfast is ready tomorrow. Don't come down until I tell you."

"Yes, Ma," said Hester. Ben looked at his father and grinned, and as Hester went up the ladder to the loft, she thought that Ben had laughed more in the last few days before Christmas than he had during the whole of the time that she had been in Silver Falls. Remembering what Mrs. Clarke had said, when she awoke on Christmas Day she lay in bed, waiting to be called. She knew that it was going to be a special breakfast because she could smell the scent of bacon frying on the stove.

"It's time to get up," Mrs. Clarke called out, and then she went into Ben's room to tell him that breakfast was ready. When Hester came down the ladder, she smiled when she glanced at the dresser. Among the plates and mugs Mrs. Clarke had arranged small red apples and sprays of dark-green fir. Below the shelves, next to Mrs. Clarke's workbasket, there was a bowl of oranges and a dish of apples, and they gleamed as if they had been polished. Although the table was set for breakfast, in the center there was a pewter mug with sprays of pine cones in it.

"It's lovely," said Hester. She looked again at the

dresser, and she thought that it was like one of the shop windows in the marketplace at Marcroft which the orphan girls passed on their way to church every Sunday morning.

"Best be sitting down for breakfast," said Mr. Clarke, but when Hester went to the table there was something on her chair. Whatever it was, it lay hidden beneath her cloak. On Ben's chair there was something covered by his jacket.

"Can we look now, Ma?" said Ben longingly. He had been told that he must wait until Hester came down into the living room before he could whisk the jacket away.

"Yes," said Mrs. Clarke, laughing.

Hester lifted up her cloak. Underneath there was a small jug and basin to stand on the chest in her own room.

"Thank you, Ma and Pa," she said. The jug and basin were decorated with a pattern of clusters of violets, and she thought that they were almost too fine for everyday use. She kissed Mr. and Mrs. Clarke, and when she glanced across at Ben, he was holding up a knife.

"Thanks, Ma and Pa," he said. "It's just what I need for when I go out in the forest." He opened another parcel in which there was a pair of shoes.

"Oh, Pa," he said. "They're just like yours." Last of all there was a long penny whistle, at which he looked with delight, and then played the scale in a lovely, clear tone.

"Aren't you going to see what else there is for you?" Mrs. Clarke said to Hester.

"Yes, Ma," Hester said. She went back to her chair and opened a big brown paper parcel. Inside there was a dress of the same rich blue fabric that she had seen on one of the shelves at Mr. Savin's store. Mrs. Clarke had made it in the evening after Hester had gone to bed.

"Thank you, Ma," said Hester. As she looked at the

dress and the jug and basin, she thought that she was the luckiest girl in the whole of Silver Falls. Even then there was another parcel to open. She unwrapped the paper and found a length of scarlet hair ribbon.

"Thank you, Ma and Pa," she said in a voice that trembled. "But what about Davy? What did he get?"

"Some new clothes," said Mrs. Clarke, "and this." She went to the cradle and held up a little horse made of some of the gray flannel that had been left over from one of Mr. Clarke's shirts. Mrs. Clarke had a new needle case, and for her husband there was a thick muffler. Hester wished that she had been able to give them a Christmas gift, but the pleasure and excitement on her face meant far more to Mr. and Mrs. Clarke than anything that might have come from Mr. Savin's store.

"It's time that we were having that breakfast," said Mr. Clarke, and they all sat down to the bacon and fried potatoes. For lunch there was roast pork, and in the afternoon they went to church in the sleigh. The Savins were there and Lottie carried a muff that had obviously been her favorite Christmas present. Mrs. Pollitt and George and Luke were there, too, and although the two young men stopped to speak to the Clarkes, Mrs. Pollitt merely said, "A merry Christmas," and then she climbed into her sleigh and sat looking straight in front of her.

Hester thought again of the missing thimble, but then she remembered the jug and basin, the blue dress, and the hair ribbon.

# Chapter 11

*A*FTER CHRISTMAS more snow fell. On the days when the blizzards raged, the people who lived on the outskirts of Silver Falls were unable to reach the village. There was a severe frost and the windows were misted with thick rime, which remained unthawed all day. Mrs. Clarke did everything possible to keep the house warm. The fire blazed in the stove. Sacks were hung against the shutters and by each door there was a curtain made of burlap.

Everyone went to bed early, and Hester sometimes thought that she wore as many clothes in bed as she did when she went to school. In addition to her nightgown she wore her shawl, a pair of Ben's socks, and a hood made from an old muffler. On the bed there were clean sacks with a thin filling of straw, her cloak, and some of the extra blankets that Mrs. Clarke had brought out from the chest in her room. In the mornings when she went up the ladder to tell Hester that it was time to get up, Mrs. Clarke took with her a jug of hot water because the water in Hester's own jug was frozen. Although Hester washed and dressed as quickly as she could, she shivered and her breath floated in the cold air like the steam from one of the big black kettles on the stove in the living room.

For breakfast there was porridge and hot milk, and on the days when she was able to go to school, she wore the muffler as well as her shawl, bonnet, and cloak. Ben had his cap and muffler, and he also wore an old jacket of his father, which was big enough to serve as an overcoat. Mrs. Clarke put a thin film of lard on the children's lips to prevent them from being cracked by the icy wind.

The snow had drifted into the hedgerows and the river was frozen. The fir trees were dark against the sky, and the branches of the trees that had shed their leaves in the fall stood bare in the wind. Hester thought that it was as if they had been blackened by fire, and she remembered the story of the phoenix which Miss Foster had told the class one afternoon. The teacher had said that the phoenix was a bird that burned itself on a funeral pyre and then rose from the ashes with renewed youth, to live again for another season. Remembering how the yellow, orange, and scarlet leaves had made the trees appear as if they were burning, Hester thought that it was as if they, too, renewed themselves through fire and then began a new life cycle in the spring.

Before Miss Foster had her breakfast she went to the schoolhouse and lit the fire in the stove so that it would be burning for at least two hours before the children arrived. When the stack of fuel in the school yard diminished, each child brought a log and some kindling every day from the wood stacked in the barns at home. All the children had coughs and chest colds. Some suffered from cold sores, and many had chilblains on their hands and feet. One morning there was a sharp rapping on the schoolhouse door and when Bill Masters went to open it, Mrs. Pollitt was waiting there. Ben was standing by Miss Foster's desk while the teacher marked the additions on his slate. He glanced at Mrs. Pollitt and then stared down the room to where Hester sat at the back of the class. There was a stern expression on his face and Hester quickly looked down again at her work and tried to go on with her arithmetic problem.

"Good morning, Mrs. Pollitt," said Miss Foster. "Please come in."

"Thank you kindly," said Mrs. Pollitt. She wiped her shoes on the sack by the door, and when she came into the room, it seemed to Hester that she had brought the icy grip of winter with her. She wondered if at long last Mrs. Pollitt had come to tell Miss Foster about the missing thimble.

"There seem to be plenty of coughs and colds about," said Mrs. Pollitt, "so I thought that it would be a good plan to keep a bottle of cough medicine right here in the schoolhouse."

From her basket she took out a large black bottle of medicine and placed it on Miss Foster's desk.

"Thank you, Mrs. Pollitt," said Miss Foster.

"And there's a bag of candy to take the taste away," said Mrs. Pollitt, as she placed a brown paper package next to the bottle.

"What do we say to Mrs. Pollitt, boys and girls?" said the teacher.

"Thank you, Mrs. Pollitt," said the class in chorus, but they were thinking of the candy and not of the medicine.

"You're welcome," said Mrs. Pollitt graciously. "Make sure that you keep well wrapped up during this cold snap, and mind that you eat everything that's put before you. Good day to you, Miss Foster."

"Good day, Mrs. Pollitt," said Miss Foster, "and thank you."

As Mrs. Pollitt went out of the room, Lottie glanced at Hester and whispered, "Even though Ma says she's done a lot of good work in Silver Falls, I always think that she's a bit scarifying, don't you?"

"No talking, Lottie," said Miss Foster sharply, "or do you want some cough medicine?"

"No, thank you, Miss Foster, ma'am," said Lottie hastily, and she bent her head over her work. The teacher was smiling as she went on marking Ben's additions.

Davy was a year old on the twenty-eighth of January, and two days after his birthday he began to walk. Mrs. Clarke held his right hand, and together they walked all around the living room while Mr. Clarke, Ben, and Hester looked on in admiration. On two occasions Davy stumbled, but he held firmly to his mother's hand and went on walking until Mrs. Clarke said, "That's enough for one day, Davy," and then she gathered him up into her arms. She looked across at Mr. Clarke, and Hester thought that there was a certain thanksgiving in her smile because in spite of all the hardships of the winter in Silver Falls, Davy was such a sturdy child.

In the letter which Miss Hayward had given to Mr. Clarke, the matron had stated that Hester's birthday was believed to be the eleventh of February. In the asylum the birthdays of the orphans had passed unnoticed by anyone except the matron, but when Hester came down the ladder from the loft into the living room on her twelfth birthday, there was a small package by her plate.

"Happy birthday, Hester," Mrs. Clarke said.

"Thank you, Ma," said Hester excitedly, and with a strange feeling in her throat she unwrapped the first birthday present that she had ever been given. It was a hairbrush.

"Oh, thank you, Ma," said Hester. She sat looking at the gift, thinking of her bedroom up in the loft. When she had arrived in Silver Falls there had been just the bed and the chest. Now, on a row of pegs, there were two aprons, her best blue dress, a blouse and skirt, and a sunbonnet. On the chest, in addition to the comb there were the matching jug and basin. Now there would be the hairbrush as well.

Soon afterward Ben came hurrying out into the living room for his breakfast.

"Happy birthday, Hester," he said, as he sat down at the table. He had been twelve in October.

"Thank you, Ben," Hester replied. She looked across at him, but the surprise and pleasure faded from her eyes when she saw that he was looking down at his plate and eating his porridge. For a moment she had hoped that this was a gesture of friendship from Ben, but then she knew that his greeting was one only of civility, and made simply because his mother was in the room. Then she looked again at the hairbrush and touched the smooth wooden back, thinking that Mrs. Clarke always seemed to know exactly what she would like to have. Hester thanked Mr. Clarke when he came home for supper, and he was pleased that the gift had given her so much happiness.

"Happy birthday, Hester," he said, looking down at her, and she remembered the first time that they had met in the low-ceilinged parlor in Mr. Weston's house in Halifax.

The thaw began at the end of March. As the snow melted and the moisture sank into the ground, the ditches were filled with swiftly flowing brown water, and the cart tracks and the streets of the village were muddy and wet. Twigs and branches were no longer tipped and weighted with ice, and in the fields, instead of the covering of snow, there was the red earth and the fresh color of the grass. In the front garden, by one of the apple trees, Mrs. Clarke found a small yellow flower, and she brought it into the house and placed it in an eggcup on the dresser.

"Now we know that the winter really is over," she said, and Hester thought of the hayrick in the yard, which had grown smaller over the weeks as the hay had been fed to Blackie and Maggie. She also thought of the number of bottles of Mrs. Pollitt's cough medicine, which had been taken in small doses by the children in the schoolhouse.

"I reckoned that one bottle would last about a week," Mrs. Pollitt had said, when she brought the second bottle.

"Thank you, Mrs. Pollitt," Miss Foster said. "I'm sure that we're all very grateful, aren't we, boys and girls?"

"Yes, Miss Foster," said the class, and Mrs. Pollitt seemed satisfied and took a paper bag of candy from her basket and gave it to the teacher. Although the children had coughs and colds, no one ever sneezed or coughed while Mrs. Pollitt was in the schoolhouse. It was almost as if her presence were as effective as the big black bottle of medicine in easing sore throats and chest colds.

Mrs. Pollitt came every week with a new bottle of medicine and a fresh supply of candy, and each time Hester was glad that her seat was at the back of the class. She had sometimes wondered what she would do if she ever were standing out in front of the class at Miss Foster's desk when Mrs. Pollitt arrived, but fortunately she had always been sitting down when the loud knocking came on the schoolhouse door. Lottie was only too ready to stop work when the visitor came, but Hester went on with her writing. Whenever she saw Mrs. Pollitt she thought of the silver thimble.

"I'm going out to see Rachel on Saturday," Lottie said one morning at school. "She asked Pa to get her some special material from Millford, and he brought it home last night. Ma said I had to take it out to her over the weekend, because Rachel doesn't see people much up where the farm is, and she's always glad of a bit of company. After that last blizzard, she and Will were snowed in for two weeks, and they didn't see a soul. Ma wondered if you'd like to go as well, Hester."

"I'll have to ask at home first," Hester said, but she thought that she would like to see Rachel and her new house.

"See what your ma says, then," said Lottie. "I expect that she'll let you come."

Hester was pleased that Lottie referred to Mrs. Clarke as her ma.

When she told Mrs. Clarke about the invitation, Mrs. Clarke said, "Of course you can go, Hester. It'll make a little outing for you." She was glad that the interest of the Savins had enabled Hester to share in some of the life of the village.

Hester arrived at the store soon after nine o'clock on Saturday. Lottie was ready with the parcel of material, and when Hester went into the living room, Mrs. Savin was packing an apple pie into a basket. From her pantry Mrs. Clarke had given Hester a jar of pickles to take to Rachel, and Mrs. Savin placed it in the basket next to the pie.

"That was very good of your ma," she said. "I know that Rachel will be pleased." She went with the two girls onto the sidewalk. "Mind that you don't stay too late," she said. "Rachel will have the afternoon milking to do, and so will you."

"All right, Ma," said Lottie cheerfully, and she and Hester set off. Hester carried the basket with the pie and the pickles, and Lottie had the parcel of material tucked under her arm.

Will and Rachel's small farm was three miles from Silver Falls, but it was a fine morning and the girls enjoyed the walk. They stood for a moment looking at the beauty of the waterfall, and then they crossed over the log bridge and went along the cart track that led to the new house.

"Soon the logs will come floating down the river from the logging camps up in the forest," Lottie said. "Then they'll be busier than ever in the lumberyard."

Mr. Clarke began work at the lumberyard at six o'clock in the morning, and Hester wondered if it was possible for anyone to be more busy than he was. Even after a day's hard work, after supper he went out to the barn and the stable, and there were always the seasonal tasks of plowing, haymaking, and harvesting.

As the two girls walked along the cart track they passed some of the land that had been cleared by Will in the months before the wedding. Roots of trees and piles of stones were silent evidence of his many hours of hard work.

"There's our Rachel," said Lottie suddenly, and in the distance they could see a figure hanging clothes on a line to dry. As they drew nearer, Rachel saw them and waved, and both Hester and Lottie waved back and hurried toward the house.

"Hello, Lottie," Rachel said. "Hello, Hester. Welcome to our home." She was pleased to see the two girls and she kissed them both. Rachel was wearing a gray blouse, a black skirt, and a blue apron. Hester thought back to the day of the wedding, and it seemed to her that Rachel looked as happy in her everyday clothes as she had on that Sunday afternoon between the haymaking and harvest time, when she wore the pink bonnet and sprigged dress and walked down the aisle of the church with Will.

"Is everybody all right at the store?" asked Rachel, as she, Hester and Lottie were walking up the garden path.

"Yes," said Lottie. "They all sent their love."

Although the house was not very large, Rachel showed them everything with a quiet pride. In the living room there was the stove, a table and four chairs, and a dresser on which stood a lamp and Rachel's workbasket. On the shelves, mugs, cups, and tin plates were arranged. In the bedroom there was a chest with a jug and basin standing on it, and the patchwork quilt covered the bed. The third room was the smallest of all, and it seemed to be filled with boxes and barrels.

"This is our storeroom for the time being," Rachel said. "Will's going to build a loft later on."

She was very pleased with the pie Mrs. Savin had sent, and with Mrs. Clarke's jar of pickles.

"Mind that you thank your ma for me," she said to Hester.

"Yes, I will, Rachel," said Hester.

Rachel also showed the girls the outbuildings. There were a barn, a cow shed, and a hen house. With the money that her Uncle Jack in Millford had given her as a wedding gift, she and Will had been able to buy some chickens and two cows.

"Will would like to have a large dairy herd one day," Rachel said. "Still, we shall have to wait and see."

Will did not come home at midday, because he was still clearing an acre of woodland. Usually Rachel had bread and cheese for her lunch, and then served the main meal of the day at suppertime, just as Mrs. Clarke did, but in honor of Lottie and Hester's visit, that day there were boiled eggs and bread and butter, followed by a slice of Mrs. Savin's pie. Lottie and Hester washed the dishes, and Rachel placed everything back on the shelves of the dresser. They all sat together in the living room until half past two, and then Lottie said that they ought to be making their way home.

"The time soon goes," said Rachel. As the two girls were putting on their bonnets and cloaks, she went into the bedroom and brought out two small pieces of material.

"Here you are, then," she said. "One piece for each of you for your patchwork."

"Thank you, Rachel," said Lottie and Hester.

The small pieces of sprigged material had been left over when Rachel made her wedding dress.

Rachel came to the farmhouse door as Hester and Lottie went down the cart track. It would soon be milking time. The two girls looked back and waved good-bye to her and then they set off for Silver Falls. Hester wondered what it would be like to be alone all day on a small farm. Then she looked down at the basket that contained the remnants of the sprigged material and she remembered the happiness on Rachel's face.

One evening everyone was in the living room. Mr. Clarke and Ben were making clothes-pegs, Mrs. Clarke was mending some socks, and Hester was busy with her patchwork. Someone knocked on the front door, and Ben went to open it.

"It's Mrs. Pollitt, Ma," he said.

"Good evening, Mrs. Pollitt," said Mrs. Clarke. She stood up, still holding the sock she had been darning. Hester sat with her patchwork, knowing that her face was red, and thinking that if Davy had not gone to sleep so quickly that evening, she would still be in the bedroom with him, and would not have seen the visitor.

"Good evening," said Mrs. Pollitt. "I was wondering if I might step inside. What I've got to say ought to be said in front of everybody."

"Come in," said Mrs. Clarke, glancing at her husband. Ben pulled a chair forward for Mrs. Pollitt, but instead of sitting down, she placed her basket on the chair and remained standing. Hester felt her hands tremble, just as they had on the night of the Christmas concert in the schoolhouse, but she went on sewing, even though the stitches were big and uneven and she would have to take them out later.

"I've come over," said Mrs. Pollitt, "to say that I've found my silver thimble."

Mr. and Mrs. Clarke and Ben glanced at Hester, but she sat at the table with her eyes downcast.

"Luke's been on for some time that he wanted to make a scarecrow for the second field," said Mrs. Pollitt. "There was nothing downstairs that he could use, so I went up into the loft to see what old clothes I had put away in the chest. While I was up there turning things over, I saw the thim-

201

ble on the shelf, shining there as large as life. It all came back to me, then. I remembered that on the day that Hester brought over the cranberries, I'd done a bit of sewing in the afternoon, and then I took it into my head to scrub the floor up in the loft. When I went up there, I still had my thimble on my finger, so I took it off and put it on the shelf for safekeeping. Too safe, you might say, after the way things have turned out. Even though I hunted high and low for it in the house, I never thought that it could be up in the loft." Her voice faltered, and after a pause she said, "I've come over to try to make amends as far as I can for what I've said and for what I've thought these past months. I've not been much of a neighbor for quite a spell." She stood with her hands clasped. "Will you look at me, Hester?" she said.

Hester had stopped sewing. She raised her head and looked at Mrs. Pollitt.

"I'm sorry for what I said," went on Mrs. Pollitt, "and I'd like to make it up to you, if I can. I'm not going to ask you to take the thimble, because even if you could ever bring yourself to use it, I dare say that it would always remind you of words that I hope that one day you will be able to forget. All the same, you're quite welcome to have the thimble, if you want it."

"No, thank you, Mrs. Pollitt," Hester said quietly. She thought of all the sewing she had done without ever possessing a thimble.

"I didn't think that you'd want it," said Mrs. Pollitt. "But I've brought something else that I hope you'll do me the honor of taking." She took a parcel from the basket and unwrapped two of the six cups and saucers that had stood on the top shelf of her dresser, and which she had said would be shared between her two sons when they married.

"When George and Luke came in to supper tonight," said Mrs. Pollitt, "I told them what had happened, what had been said, and what had been thought, and they were agreeable that I should bring two of the cups and saucers over to you."

Hester thought of the worry that there had been for Mr. and Mrs. Clarke, and of the way in which Ben had looked at her after Mrs. Pollitt had said that the thimble was missing from its case. She remembered how she was afraid that she might be sent back to England, to a reformatory, and she thought of the Christmas concert when she had nearly spoiled the Bible reading because the sight of Mrs. Pollitt sitting in the audience had unnerved her. For a moment it seemed to her that she had been punished almost as if she really had taken the silver thimble.

There was silence in the room as everyone waited to hear what she would say. She looked at Mrs. Pollitt's hands and saw how she held them clasped tightly in front of her, just as the girls at the asylum stood and waited for Miss Brown to pass judgment on their sewing. Mrs. Pollitt had come to put things right and to make amends, regardless of what it would cost her. She had been honest and courageous enough to admit her mistake in front of everyone. That would always be a real test of a person's strength of character. Hester stood up.

"I'm glad that you've found your thimble, Mrs. Pollitt," she said. "But as for the cups and saucers, well, they're so pretty, I . . ." Then she was unable to say anything more, but rushed over to where Mrs. Clarke was standing and hugged her.

"Oh, Ma," she said.

"All right, Hester," said Mrs. Clarke, as she stroked the fair hair. "Everything's all right."

She looked at her neighbor. "Will you sit down and have a cup of tea, Mrs. Pollitt?" she said.

"Well, not tonight," said Mrs. Pollitt in a shaking voice. "But perhaps in a day or two, or when your girl here would be willing."

She laid her big red hand on Hester's shoulder for a moment. "Good night," she said.

Ben opened the door for her.

"I'm obliged to you all," said Mrs. Pollitt, and then she went out and climbed up into the buggy and drove away.

After school the next day, Hester walked up the cart track to Pollitt's Spread. She had intended to go around to the back door, just as she had done when she had taken the basket of cranberries to the farmhouse, but on this occasion Mrs. Pollitt looked out from the window of the living room and saw her coming. She opened the front door and stood waiting for her on the porch.

"Thank you," she said gently. "Step inside."

In the evening when Mrs. Clarke and Hester were alone in the living room, Hester said, "Would you like to have the cups and saucers, Ma? There's not a crack or chip on them." She smiled as she looked at the china on the dresser, thinking that she must sound just like Mrs. Pollitt.

"That's very kind of you, Hester," said Mrs. Clarke, "but Mrs. Pollitt brought them for you, and now they're yours. You can keep them safely up in your room. Perhaps one day you'll have a place of your own, and they'll come in useful then."

"All right, Ma," said Hester, but she thought that the only place she wanted to be was with Mr. and Mrs. Clarke and Davy, and even with Ben.

# Chapter 12

"DID YOU HEAR the rain in the night?" asked Mrs. Clarke one morning when Ben and Hester were having their breakfast.

"Yes," said Ben. "I woke up once and it seemed to be just pouring down."

"Pa was wondering about the roof on the barn," said Mrs. Clarke. "He's going to have a look at it this evening. Did the rain keep you awake, Hester?"

"Yes," Hester replied. "It came so hard against the window that I thought it might break the glass." She had lain warm and comfortable in her bed in the loft, thankful that she was not out in the storm.

"I was thinking about the blankets," said Mrs. Clarke, smiling. "I'd made up my mind that I really must get on with washing them this morning. Still, I think I'll be able to, after all. It looks as if the sun's going to shine through."

Several times during lessons Hester glanced out of the window and on one occasion she was reprimanded by Miss Foster, but she was glad that it was a fine day and that Mrs. Clarke would be able to wash the blankets. It was her week to do the afternoon milking, so as soon as school had ended she hurried back to the Clarkes' house. When she reached the gate she could see that the four blankets were hung out to dry on the clothesline in the front garden. Mrs. Clarke was weeding her flower bed, and Davy was playing on the porch. His mother had made a harness for him, which was tied to one of the posts to prevent him from wandering off.

"It's been a good drying day, after all, Hester," Mrs. Clarke said, and Hester knew that she was pleased. She gave Davy a kiss and then hurried into the living room for the milking cap and apron, and when she went out to the small field Maggie was already waiting by the gate.

When the milking was done, Hester set the two pitchers to cool in the tub of water and then scoured the milking pail and put it out to dry in the sunlight. Then she went to the front porch and stood looking at Davy, who seemed to be absorbed in a game with two sticks and three stones.

Ben had arrived home from school and was busy raking over a part of the garden in readiness for the time when Mr. Clarke's seedlings could be transplanted. Hester went over to the narrow strip of flower garden and began to help Mrs. Clarke with the weeding. She always enjoyed gardening and would really have liked to have a little plot of her own, but every foot of the garden had been freed from brushwood and undergrowth by Mr. Clarke when he and his wife had first come to live in Silver Falls, and she knew that most of the hard-won soil must be used for growing food. The heavy rain throughout the night had beaten some of the plants to the ground.

"These will need staking," Mrs. Clarke said, looking at her yellow daisies. "Would you bring me the twine from the dresser, Hester, please?"

"Yes, Ma," Hester said. She ran up the steps to the porch and went into the living room for the twine, which was kept in the second drawer of the dresser. When she came out from the house, she looked down the path. The gate at the beginning of the cart track was being opened by someone wearing a gray dress who moved very slowly, as if each step she took were made possible only by a great effort. At first Hester thought that it was an old woman, but it was the gray dress that made her stare in disbelief. She would have known it anywhere. It was the uniform of the institution.

"Bethanne!" she called, and ran to meet her friend, but her smile of welcome faded when she saw Bethanne's white face and the deep shadows under her eyes. There was a rent in one of the sleeves of her dress, and the skirt was splashed with mud. The dress hung on her loosely, just as it had when she had put it on for the first time in the sewing room of the orphan asylum.

"Please let me stay," Bethanne murmured. She took a slow, painful step forward, and would have fallen if Hester had not reached out and held her. She looked down at Bethanne's thin, drawn face, and at the damp, tangled hair, and she was afraid.

"Ma!" she called out, but Mrs. Clarke and Ben were already hurrying down the path.

"It's Bethanne, Ma," said Hester, when Mrs. Clarke was beside her. "We came from England together."

"All right, Hester," said Mrs. Clarke, and her quiet tone steadied Hester as she took Bethanne from her.

"Run over and ask Mrs. Pollitt to come, Ben," Mrs. Clarke said. "Be as quick as you can."

"Yes, Ma," said Ben, and he ran off to Pollitt's Spread, thinking how different Hester in her brown dress seemed from the girl with the big, staring eyes in the gray uniform. Hester followed Mrs. Clarke as she carried Bethanne up to the house and into the bedroom, where she laid her on the big bed and began to unlace her shoes. Hester knelt by the bedside, but Bethanne lay with her eyes closed. When Mrs. Clarke took off the shoe, they could see that Bethanne was not wearing stockings, and that the sole of her foot was covered with red, broken blisters.

"Put two kettles on the stove, Hester," Mrs. Clarke said, "and make some broth."

"Yes, Ma," Hester said, and although she really wanted to stay by the bed, she went out into the living room and filled the two big kettles and put them on the stove, wondering how her friend had come all the way from Mapletown. She thought of Bethanne's damp hair and the state of her dress, and she wondered if she had been out in the storm during the night.

George Pollitt was repairing the roof of the front porch at Pollitt's Spread as Ben came running up the cart track. He climbed down the ladder, sensing that something was wrong.

"Easy, now, Ben," he said, when Ben reached the porch. "What's happened?"

"Can Mrs. Pollitt come?" said Ben. His face was very red and he was breathing heavily. "A girl's just walked in home from off the road. She's in a bad way."

"Ma's inside," said George. He opened the front door and went with Ben into the living room, where Mrs. Pollitt was ironing.

"It seems that you're needed up at the Clarkes' place, Ma," said George. "I'll bring the buggy around to the front."

"What is it, Ben?" said Mrs. Pollitt, putting down her flatiron. She listened to what he had to say, and then she went to her special cupboard where she kept her medicines, ointments, and bandages, and began to pack some things into a basket. When she was ready, she and Ben went out to the front porch, where George was waiting with the horse and buggy.

"You can drive, Ben," said Mrs. Pollitt, as she stepped up into the buggy. "I may be late," she said to George. "The potatoes are ready in the saucepan, and there's a pie on the second shelf of the pantry."

"All right, Ma," said George. It would not be the first time that only he and Luke had sat at the supper table because Mrs. Pollitt had been asked to visit someone who was ill.

When Hester had warmed some broth, she poured it into a basin and carried it into the bedroom.

"Right," said Mrs. Clarke. "Put your arm around Bethanne while she has the broth."

Hester supported Bethanne while Mrs. Clarke held the spoon to her lips, but she was able to swallow only a little of the broth before she began to cough, making a harsh, choking sound, which frightened Hester. She thought how small her friend seemed, lying in the big bed, wearing one of Mrs. Clarke's nightgowns. The gray dress and her underclothes lay on the floor, just where Mrs. Clarke had dropped them. When the coughing stopped, Bethanne had difficulty in breathing. Every breath she took was like a sigh.

"Good afternoon, Mrs. Clarke," said Mrs. Pollitt calmly, when she came into the bedroom, and Hester felt that everything was going to be all right now that she was there.

"Will you go and wait for the kettles to boil, Hester?" Mrs. Pollitt said, and Hester nodded and went out to the living room. Ben was standing by the front door, but she stood with her back to him, just looking at the two kettles, remembering that Bethanne had given no sign that she had recognized her. She wished that there were something she could do to help. She looked up quickly when Mrs. Clarke came out from the bedroom, but she spoke to Ben.

"Mrs. Pollitt wants you to take the buggy and go into Millford for Dr. Hall, Ben," she said. "It's the house by the church."

"Yes, Ma," said Ben, and he hurried out to the buggy and drove off. Mrs. Clarke went back into the bedroom, but before she shut the door, Hester was able to hear the sound of Bethanne's coughing. She wished that she were older, so that she could be in the bedroom with the grown-ups, not being afraid, but knowing what to do, just as Mrs. Pollitt knew. She stood by the stove, thinking that the kettles would never boil, but at last they did and she knocked on the bedroom door and waited for Mrs. Clarke to come out for them.

"Is there anything I can do, Ma?" she said desperately.

"Bethanne's in good hands," said Mrs. Clarke, "and the doctor will be here as soon as he can. Just see that Davy's not getting into any mischief, and then make a start on supper."

"All right, Ma," said Hester. She went out to the front porch to see what Davy was doing. He looked up and smiled at her, and then went on playing with his sticks and stones, so she went back into the living room and began to peel the potatoes for supper. It was very quiet and sometimes she could hear the sound of coughing and the murmur of voices, and she wondered what was happening in the bedroom. She put the saucepan of potatoes on the stove and began to lay the table, setting two extra places in case Mrs. Pollitt and Doctor Hall stayed to supper.

Mr. Clarke came home first and he looked grave when she told him what had happened, and then Mrs. Clarke came into the living room, carrying Davy's cradle. She and her husband went out to the front porch for a few minutes, and then Mrs. Clarke went back into the bedroom, and Mr. Clarke put the cradle in Ben's room.

Hester went on with the supper, but when it was ready, only Mr. Clarke sat down at the table. Hester took Davy on her lap and gave him his bread and milk. She was making some tea when Ben and Dr. Hall arrived. The doctor went into the bedroom, and before the door was shut, Hester could again hear the sound of coughing.

"All right, Ben?" said Mr. Clarke.

"Yes, Pa," Ben said, but he looked tired.

"Come and have your supper," said Mr. Clarke.

Ben sat down at the table, and Hester took his meal from the oven and placed it before him.

"Thanks," he said. She filled his mug with tea, and then began to get Davy ready for bed, hoping that he would go to sleep quickly, and not find it strange being in Ben's room. There was a dull ache in her throat and she felt unable to sing that evening. She tucked Davy up in the cot and sat watching him. He was restless at first, knowing that he was in a different room, but she talked soothingly to him and then he gradually settled down to sleep.

In the other bedroom Bethanne told her story, although she never knew if anyone heard it. She lay in the big bed, reliving the events of the past few days, and though sometimes her mind wandered, Dr. Hall, Mrs. Clarke and Mrs. Pollitt were able to piece together what had happened.

Bethanne had found little understanding with the Giffords. At the isolated farmhouse she had been expected to do the work of a full-grown woman, but Mr. Gifford had been a strange, silent man, and his wife was grudging and impatient, always ready with angry words when she found fault with what Bethanne did.

Bethanne had tried very hard to please them. In spite of her fear of the cows, she had learned to milk. She had scrubbed the floors in the farmhouse, chopped wood and worked in the fields, even walking behind the plow, but never had there been one word of praise or encouragement. Her cough had steadily worsened. One afternoon at milking time, a cow had kicked the milking pail, and the milk ran all over the floor of the cow shed, and it was then, because she was afraid to tell Mrs. Gifford what had happened, that she decided to run away.

The only place she knew was the Clarkes' house at Silver Falls, and it seemed a long time ago that she had sat in the living room with Hester, eating the bread and butter which Mrs. Clarke had placed on the table. Bethanne had never had butter on her bread at the Giffords' farm.

Without really knowing how far it was, she had set out for Silver Falls, going into the forest because she thought that if she ran along the road, Mr. Gifford would follow her in the buggy and take her back. She had lost her way among all the trees, bushes, and bracken, but she still went on until it was dark, and then she was so weary that she was only too glad to lie down and rest.

She had wandered for two days, finding only leaves to eat. During the storm she crouched beneath the bracken, trying to find shelter from the rain, and in the morning when the sun rose, it seemed like a miracle when at last she came to the edge of the forest and saw the road. Slowly she had walked until she came to the Clarkes' house.

Bethanne began to cough again, and Dr. Hall nodded to Mrs. Pollitt, who gave her some more of the medicine which the doctor had brought. Mrs. Clarke picked up the wet shoes, the underclothes, and the mud-stained gray dress and went out into the living room, just as Hester was closing the door of Ben's bedroom.

"Is she going to be all right, Ma?" said Hester.

"Bethanne's come a long way," replied Mrs. Clarke. "She's very tired."

"Why did she come here, Ma?" said Ben.

"Because this was the only place she could think of," said Mrs. Clarke.

Hester said nothing, but she looked at the asylum uniform and thought of the day when her dress had been dyed brown and Mrs. Clarke had allowed her to choose the yellow trimming.

"Is Davy asleep, Hester?" asked Mrs. Clarke.

"Yes, Ma," Hester said. She wanted to know more of what had happened, but she felt that this was not the time to ask.

Dr. Hall came into the living room and they all waited to hear what he had to say.

"I'll come again tomorrow, Mrs. Clarke," he said. "I've left some things with Mrs. Pollitt. She'll tell you what to do."

"Thank you, Doctor," said Mrs. Clarke. "Will you have something to eat before you go?"

"No, thank you, ma'am," said Dr. Hall, "not just now."

Mrs. Clarke nodded. She was not hungry, either. She and Mr. Clarke followed the doctor out to the front porch and stayed talking for a few moments before Dr. Hall drove back to Millford. Hester began to clear the table, unaware that Ben was looking at her.

Mrs. Pollitt stayed until eight o'clock. "I'll be over first thing in the morning," she said. "Bethanne's sleeping now, and a good night's rest can make a world of difference."

Mrs. Clarke spent the night in the chair in the big bedroom and Mr. Clarke slept on the floor in the living room. In her bed in the loft, Hester lay looking up at the rafters, remembering how hard it had rained the night before. It was a long time before she went to sleep, but the next morning she was awake early and could hear Mr. Clarke moving about in the living room. As soon as he had gone to work, she washed and dressed and went down the ladder. Mrs. Clarke was sitting in the rocking chair, with her hands folded in her lap, and she looked up in surprise when she heard Hester's footsteps.

"I was awake, so I thought that I might as well get up," Hester said, but Mrs. Clarke saw the questioning look in her eyes.

"Bethanne's still asleep," she said.

"How are you, Ma?" said Hester.

"I'll be all right," said Mrs. Clarke, but Hester thought that she looked tired.

"Do you mind staying home from school today?" Mrs. Clarke asked. "I'd like you to look after Davy."

"All right, Ma," Hester said. "I'll see to Ben's breakfast."

"Thank you, Hester," said Mrs. Clarke, and then she went into the big bedroom and closed the door. Hester sat in the rocking chair until it was time to make the porridge, and when it was ready, she knocked on Ben's door. She knew that his mother always had to call him three or even four times before he answered, but she thought that he must have been awake early, too, because he said, "All right," after she had knocked only once. He went up to the loft to wash, and while he had his breakfast, Hester wrapped some bread and cheese in a cloth for his lunch. He was lacing up his shoes when Mrs. Clarke came into the living room.

"Hester's not going to school today, Ben," she said. "I want you to tell Miss Foster that I need her here at home."

"Yes, Ma," said Ben. He picked up his lunch from the table and went off to school. Hester was giving Davy his breakfast when Mrs. Pollitt drove up in the buggy, and she went to the door with Davy in her arms.

"Good morning, Mrs. Pollitt," she said.

"Good morning, Hester," said Mrs. Pollitt. "And you, young man," she said, touching Davy on his cheek. Dr. Hall came soon afterward, and Hester thought that everyone must have been up early that morning. She washed the breakfast things and went on with the housework, thinking how quiet it was in the house, and wondering what was happening in the big bedroom.

It was just after ten o'clock when Mrs. Pollitt came into the living room.

"Go in now, Hester," she said gently. "I'll stay and look after Davy."

Hester went into the bedroom, and as she stood by the bedside, Mrs. Clarke put her arm round her. At first she thought that Bethanne was sleeping, because she breathed so deeply, but then her eyes opened and she looked at Hester.

"Hello, Bethanne," said Hester.

"Hester," whispered Bethanne, and she smiled.

"You'll be all right," Hester said, but she remembered that it was what she had also told her friend on the day that Bethanne had driven away in the buggy with Mr. Gifford. She thought of the evening at the asylum when Miss Fitch had led the bewildered and frightened girl in to supper, and as she listened to the harsh sound of Bethanne's breathing, she wanted to help and comfort her, just as she had when she was eight years old, but only Dr. Hall could do that now. I have been given so much, she thought, and Bethanne has had so little. Then she realized how quiet it was in the room.

"I'm sorry, my dear," said Doctor Hall.

Hester looked at Mrs. Clarke.

"Ma?" she said questioningly, but Mrs. Clarke held her very close and took her out from the room, and she knew that Bethanne had died. Mrs. Pollitt went into the bedroom and closed the door.

"We'll see that justice is done," Dr. Hall said, before he drove back to Millford, but Hester thought that whatever happened, it would be too late to help Bethanne. Even after she had cried, there was a dragging pain in her throat, and she felt cold, as if instead of springtime it were the middle of winter, with ice and snow everywhere.

"I must get back, I suppose," Mrs. Pollitt said, later in the morning.

"Thank you for all that you've done," said Mrs. Clarke.

"It was little enough anyone could do," said Mrs. Pollitt. She glanced at Hester, who sat with Davy on her lap. "I'll ask George and Luke to come over tonight," she said quietly.

"Thank you," said Mrs. Clarke, and then her neighbor drove home to Pollitt's Spread.

At midday Mrs. Clarke put bread and cheese on the table, but only Davy was able to eat anything. In the afternoon Mr. Anderson came, and Hester and Mrs. Clarke knelt on the floor of the living room while he said prayers for Bethanne. He spoke kindly to Hester, and although she answered as respectfully as she could, the pain in her throat was still there. When it was milking time, she took her cap and apron from the peg.

"Ben can do the milking when he comes home from school, Hester," Mrs. Clarke said. "He'll be here soon."

"I'll do it, Ma," Hester said. As she went out to the small field she remembered her own feelings when for a few moments she had thought that she was lost among the thickets of bracken and the towering trees in the forest. She sighed, and then opened the gate for Maggie. When Hester had finished the milking and was walking back across the yard, she glanced at the window of the big bedroom. The curtains were drawn. Ben was in the living room with Mrs. Clarke and Davy, and she knew from the expression on his face that his mother had told him what had happened.

She saw how tired Mrs. Clarke looked, and she helped her as much as she could when it was time to get supper, thinking that some comfort was to be gained from doing the ordinary, everyday things. Ben sat looking out of the window, and when he said, "There's Pa," Mrs. Clarke went out onto the front porch and waited for her husband. There was no need for her to say anything. When Mr. Clarke came into the living room he was very gentle with Hester, and she tried hard not to cry. He put his hand under her chin and looked down at her, and then she said, "Oh, Pa," and pressed her face against the rough cloth of his coat. "There, now, Hester," he said. They all tried to eat some supper, but no one seemed very hungry. George and Luke came, and they went with Mr. Clarke into the barn. Hester put Davy to bed in Ben's room, and although he lay in his cradle watching her for a long time, she was unable to sing the lullaby. When at last he was asleep, she went into the living room. Ben was whittling a piece of wood and Mrs. Clarke was sewing. Hester took out her patchwork, but she made little progress, and she was glad when it was time to go to bed.

"Where are you going to sleep, Ma?" she said, when Mrs. Clarke was tucking the blankets around her.

"Never mind about me," said Mrs. Clarke.

On the day that Bethanne was buried, the sun shone and the sky was blue. Ben went to school, but Mr. Clarke came home from work at midday. Mrs. Clarke picked all the spring flowers in her garden, and when Mrs. Pollitt drove up with George and Luke, she was carrying some apple blossom. George and Luke had come for the funeral, and Mrs. Pollitt took Hester and Davy back to Pollitt's Spread.

"You can make some candy, if you like," she said. "I'm

getting a bit low. I'll show you my special recipe, which I've never told anyone before."

"Thank you, Mrs. Pollitt," said Hester.

"Shall we see them go by first?" said Mrs. Pollitt.

"Yes, please," said Hester. They stood by the window and after a few minutes they saw the horse and cart pass by. Mr. Clarke and George and Luke were sitting at the front, and Mrs. Clarke sat in the back of the cart, wearing a black shawl over her hair.

"Now we'll see about that candy," said Mrs. Pollitt. "Folk seem to like it far more than they do my medicine."

Hester did everything that Mrs. Pollitt told her, and when the candy had cooled, it was the same rich, golden color as if Mrs. Pollitt had made it herself.

"You're quick to learn," said Mrs. Pollitt. "I reckon you'll make somebody a fine wife one day."

While Mrs. Pollitt did some ironing, Hester sat on the floor and played with Davy, but all the time she was thinking of Bethanne. When Mr. and Mrs. Clarke and George and Luke came back, Ben was with them.

"Has Davy been a good boy, Hester?" said Mrs. Clarke.

"Yes, Ma," said Hester. She thought how pale Mrs. Clarke's face seemed against the folds of the black shawl.

"They haven't been a morsel of trouble," Mrs. Pollitt said. "It seems a long time ago that I had a boy of Davy's age in my house, and I never had the chance of a daughter before."

She went with them to the front porch and held Davy while Hester and Mrs. Clarke climbed up into the cart, and then she put Davy into his mother's arms.

"Thank you, Mrs. Pollitt," Hester said, "for everything."

"God bless you," said Mrs. Pollitt, and then Mr. Clarke drove the family home. When Hester went into the living room, the door of Mrs. Clarke's bedroom was wide open, and she stood on the threshold, looking in. The curtains had been drawn back, and the sunlight shone through the window on the floorboards and the patchwork quilt. There was nothing in the room to remind anyone of what had happened there.

It was milking time, so she put on her cap and apron. In the cow shed she sat with her head against Maggie's flank and pressed the warm, rich milk into the pail, while the cow stood contentedly eating the hay.

"Is everything all right, Hester?" asked Mr. Clarke. He had been standing by the cow shed door for a long time before Hester looked up.

"Yes, thank you, Pa," she said, and he nodded and went into the barn.

When the milking was done, she went back to the house. Mrs. Clarke, Davy, and Ben were in the living room.

"Ma," Hester said. "Can I go down to the graveyard, please?"

"Do you really want to, Hester?" said Mrs. Clarke softly. "It's been a long day for all of us. I thought that we'd have an early supper."

"Please, Ma," Hester said. It was the first time that she had ever asked for anything.

Even though Ben was in the room, she wanted to tell Mrs. Clarke of what she had been thinking ever since Bethanne had been carried into the house, still wearing the gray uniform of the Marcroft orphan asylum.

"When the arrangements were made in England for the six of us to come to Nova Scotia," she said, "I don't know who decided that I should live here with you and Mr. Clarke, but it could have happened that I might have been sent to the Giffords instead of Bethanne, and then . . ." Her voice faltered, and she held the back of a chair to steady herself. "That's why I'd like to go, Ma," she said.

"All right, Hester," Mrs. Clarke replied, and she went to the row of pegs and took down Hester's bonnet and shawl.

"Don't be too long," she said.

"No, Ma," said Hester. "Thank you."

Mrs. Clarke stood on the porch as Hester walked slowly to the gate. Then she sighed and went back into the living room and began to prepare supper.

As Hester walked past Pollitt's Spread, Mrs. Pollitt was at the window of the living room, and she knew where she was going. After supper, she would go down into the village, too.

In the graveyard at the side of the church, Hester looked down at the white cross that Mr. Clarke had made for Bethanne. Beside the spring flowers and the apple blossom, there were flowers from Lottie's garden and fronds of young, green bracken, which the women of Silver Falls had brought to the church for the girl, who, a little more than a year ago, had passed through the main street of their village, on her way to what she believed would be a new and happy life. It was then that Hester cried, and the tears brought a kind of relief to the ache in her throat.

After a while she went across to the picket fence and looked at the dark outline of the trees, thinking of her gentle friend who had found the courage to come alone through the forest. She thought of Kitty Andrews, Ellen Holt, Mary Lewis, and Mercy Skinner, who had also walked down the gangway of the *Annapolis Valley* to a new life in a new land, wearing the uniform of the Marcroft orphan asylum, and carrying their few possessions wrapped in a black shawl. She would never know if they found a true home, such as she had, or whether there were times when they wished themselves back in the sewing room with Miss Brown at the asylum.

She thought of Mr. and Mrs. Clarke, and of all the things they had done for her, just as if she really were their own daughter. She knew how fortunate she was. Even if Ben would never accept her, she would try to understand the way he felt.

It would be different with Davy, because as far back as he would be able to remember, she would always have been there as part of the family. When Davy was old enough to understand, Ben would probably tell him that she was not his real sister at all, but was just someone who had come from an orphan asylum. Even if Ben doesn't tell him, she thought, I shall, so that Davy will know what his parents have done for me.

Slowly she walked back to Bethanne's grave and looked again at the white cross. "Good night, Bethanne," Hester said. She walked along the graveyard path and set out for home. Tomorrow she would go to school.

As she passed the side road that led to the schoolhouse, she wondered what she would do when she was grown up, and then she remembered how she had felt as she waited for the two kettles to boil. She had wished then that she knew how to help people when they were sick, just as Mrs. Pollitt knew. Perhaps one day Mrs. Pollitt would let her read the books that Doctor Hall had given to her and which were kept on the top shelf of the special cupboard. While she was still at school she would work hard and try to learn everything Miss Foster could teach her, and when it was time for her to leave school, she would tell Ma that she wanted to be able to help people when they were ill. If Mrs. Clarke agreed with her plan, perhaps she would speak to Mrs. Pollitt, and she might even drive into Millford and see Dr. Hall.

Hester walked up the path to the Clarkes' house, thinking of the day when she had seen it for the first time, the day she and Bethanne had driven along the cart track with Mr. Clarke. A horse and buggy had been by the hitching rail, and Ben had been waiting on the front porch.

Only Ben was there this time, and when he saw her, instead of going inside the house as he had on that first afternoon, he sat quite still. When Hester reached the porch, he stood up, and she felt the color rise in her face. For a moment she hesitated, and then she looked down and began to unpin her shawl, so that he would go in to supper first.

But he had opened the door and was waiting for her to go into the living room.

"Thank you," she murmured.

"You're welcome," said Ben.